MW01592825

Toads and Nettles

November 2007

To Norman, from a
would-be writer to a
professional ... You were
a real inspiration to my
students!
Susan

Toads and Nettles

Memories of the Northwest Coast

Susan Bowers

Copyright © 2004 by Susan Bowers.

ISBN :   Softcover   1-4134-4754-6

To order additional copies of this book, contact:
Xlibris Corporation
1-888-795-4274
www.Xlibris.com
Orders@Xlibris.com
23988

Contents

THIS STORY COMMEMORATES
A WAY OF LIFE THAT FEW PEOPLE
HAVE EXPERIENCED.
NAMES AND SITUATIONS
HAVE BEEN CHANGED
TO PROTECT THE GUILTY.

Chapter One

Blubber Bay

It was the last week of August, 1982, and I sat buckled into a small floatplane headed toward one of the most isolated teaching posts on the B.C. coast. If ever I had wanted adventure, this was surely my chance to get it. Isolation in itself was nothing new to me; my first teaching job ever had been in a remote logging camp, and since then I had lived and taught in other small, out-of-the-way communities. However, none of them approached the situation I was getting into now.

I hadn't learned much yet about Blubber Bay, just enough to know that it had a permanent population of eleven people, with no access in or out except by boat or float plane. There would be no telephone, and no T.V. reception. There weren't even any roads; my students would be delivered each morning by boat.

The plane flew over endless little forested islands. There was no sign of human habitation anywhere. I searched the ocean and the wilderness beneath us for some indication that people lived or worked in all that vast land, but there was nothing. Not a fish boat to be seen chugging slowly over the wrinkled grey ocean, and no lonely cabins hidden in some reclusive bay. No logged hillsides, no gravel roads, not even another plane. Just hundreds of uninhabited and uninhabitable islets, a labyrinth of channels, and not even a seagull to mar the featureless immensity of it all.

My attention was distracted by the pilot as he tapped my arm and pointed out the far window. Peering past him, I could see a doughnut-shaped rainbow glimmering over a small white cloud. I must have looked surprised, for shouting over the roar of the engine, the pilot explained briefly, "Sun dog!" I had never seen such a thing before, nor even knew they existed. But the sun dog was soon behind us, and my eyes returned to the monotonous landscape ahead.

I had a good view from the passenger's seat beside the pilot. The seats behind us had been removed to accommodate my luggage. There were a few boxes of books, a four-month supply of food, and a couple of boxes of household paraphernalia back there, a suitcase of clothes, and a heavy yellow dingy with two oars. All of this barely covered the floor on one side of the plane, and I wondered if I should have brought more in with me. We planned to live simply, but it looked like very little to be moving into a new home with.

My husband Richard, finishing a job contract in Victoria, wouldn't be joining me until Christmas. Our ten-year-old daughter Donna remained with her father to give me a chance to settle in. Richard would drive her to Kelsey Bay and put her aboard an airplane in four days' time. Until then I was on my own. The separation added to my sense of impending isolation. It was the first time we had been apart since our marriage twelve years earlier.

As we flew on and on I thought back to how I had got into this position, leaving home, family, and friends for a job that seemed like a wild leap into professional oblivion. It was Richard who had discovered the small ad in the Victoria paper. He was working at that time as a camera salesman, a job which in his words "made the soul grow small." It brought in barely enough to live on, and left Richard too few hours for writing or music or the never-ending maintenance on the boat that was our home.

As for me, I was willing to consider any alternative to my job as a substitute teacher. Permanent, full-time jobs were not easy to come by, so the advertisement placed by the North Island

School Board held hope of better times for both of us. *Teacher wanted for one-room school*, it had read. *Must have own boat.* In a time of rampant budget cutbacks and teacher layoffs, this was too good an opportunity to pass up. We didn't have much time to discuss the pros and cons of the decision: How would we adapt as a family to the profound isolation? What would Richard do with his time? What of Donna's French and violin lessons? My application was on its way in the next mail, and within a week I had a phone call asking me for an interview.

The drive up-island for the interview had been a familiar one. When I first started teaching at the north of Vancouver Island before my marriage, the trip had included several onerous and exhausting hours of driving on winding, ill-graded logging roads. By this time, however, a paved highway ran straight from Victoria in the south to Port Hardy at the northern tip of the island. Halfway up the island, the town of Campbell River marked a boundary between civilized south and wild north. Campbell River has a curious status to people living on the coast. To British Columbians who have only known the comforts of Victoria and Vancouver it is the far north, marking the furthermost reaches of cultivated farmland and hospitable, rolling hills. To those who live beyond, however, where the mountains become stark and forbidding, and shrouded with impenetrable forests, the town is synonymous with civilization, and we were eventually to meet many people who had never been south of that frontier.

Six hours of driving left Campbell River far behind as I entered Port Hardy shortly after noon. A town of some five thousand inhabitants, it is considered large by the standards of people who live there. It didn't take much time to find the larger of the town's two elementary schools, where I was to meet my principal-to-be, Frank Weston. Frank had a reputation as a tough administrator which was born out by his appearance. Lean and fit with greying hair and a pugnacious jaw, he had a no-nonsense air. But my interview with him was more of a formality than a hurdle since with ten thousand unemployed teachers in the province, there had been only two contenders for this job; myself and an unqualified secondary teacher.

Frank stood as I was ushered into his office and extended a large, muscular hand. "Pleased to meet you," he said. "So you're the lady who dares the wilderness. I've been talking to Brian about you—" this was a former principal of mine—"and he thinks you'll work out just fine."

"That's reassuring," I answered. "I don't know anything about Blubber Bay, though. I've heard of it, of course, but I thought those out-lying schools had pretty much all been shut down."

"They have, with two exceptions," Frank said. "Blubber Bay is one of them, and they've kept their student numbers well over the minimum of ten students. There are twenty kids there now."

"Grades one to seven?"

"I believe there's at least one or two students in each grade. I have a class list here somewhere." Frank scrabbled through a pile of loose papers on his desk. "Yes, here it is, on the month-end report. Would you like to see it?"

I took the proffered paper and studied the unfamiliar names that would soon take on faces and personalities. There was a heavy concentration of students in the middle grades, which would work out well for our daughter Donna. But the list included both a student at the kindergarten level, and another in grade 8.

"This is a wide spread," I commented, "K to Eight."

"You don't have to take the kindergarten child," Frank hastened to assure me. "Most teachers don't; they find it too much to handle. But the boy is from a good family. And as for the oldest student, he's just biding his time until he can drop out. In a few more months he'll be old enough to get a job in the logging camp."

That didn't speak well for student motivation. I handed back the list of names and settled into my chair. "There are a lot of things I'd like to know about Blubber Bay," I said, "but first, why did the last teacher leave?"

"In his case there were a couple of good reasons. His wife has been quite sick, and of course there's no medical attention out there. He had a bit of trouble with his neighbors, too, nothing too serious. I advised him to stick it out, but with the wife to worry about he didn't want to try."

"What kind of trouble?"

"The usual sort of thing. The poor fellow brought it on himself. There are always cliques in a little place like Blubber Bay, and a teacher can't allow himself to be drawn in. In this case there was some kind of disagreement in the community, and he took sides. Now he has enemies there. It's as simple as that."

"What kind of disagreement?"

"It was never made too clear. Discipline on the school boat was part of it. There's one fellow who has a grant to drive all the kids to school, and I guess there are some parents who would rather take their kids themselves. Nothing like this should concern the teacher though. Until they step onto school property it's not the teacher's business what the community chooses to fight about."

"What happened to the teacher before him?" I asked.

"Ah, that was Merv!" Frank grimaced. "He was a free-school philosopher, and the community is very conservative. They didn't take too well to the kids running the school and calling the teacher by his first name. When I went over there in the late spring the place was bedlam, with Merv on the edge of a breakdown. He didn't last out the year."

"So you want a teacher with a conservative style, who doesn't take sides," I observed. "And the teacher before that?"

"Well, that was an unusual case. The whole family became ill. They blamed it on the water—the run-off, you know—but it's been tested since and it's really quite safe."

"Well we're all healthy, and I'm not going to go looking for trouble in the community." I was sure that I could handle the social dynamics and physical challenges of Blubber Bay. Little did I know that the community thrived on vendetta, and that it would be inescapable.

#

I was jolted back to the present as the pilot tapped my arm

again and the plane started circling lower. I hadn't realized that we were approaching Blubber Bay, but now as I looked through the window I could see signs of habitation for the first time since we had left Kelsey Bay almost an hour earlier. A number of rustic-looking buildings hugged the shore, some of them on land but others actually floating in the water. A rickety assemblage of docks with a large shed lay to the right, with a few small boats tied up to it. On the other side of the bay, a weathered jetty sloped steeply down to the water.

The engine roared as the plane came in for a landing at the mouth of the bay, then with a small bump we were down. We motored sedately toward the lone jetty while I peered around. From this vantage point it was easier to see our surroundings. Beyond the docks on our right, two buildings nestled among the trees, one right at the waterfront, and the other up a well maintained path. Ahead of us, to our left, three cedar float-houses were tethered to the shore with a network of logs. Still further up the bay, a well-worn boat house sat on a white shell beach.

The pilot cut the engine and stepped out onto the floats as we drifted silently up to the dock. I was impressed, knowing how difficult it could be to bring a boat into dock at just the right speed and angle. The plane had just enough momentum to take it alongside the jetty. Stepping from the pontoon, the pilot tied the plane then opened the door to unload my cargo.

"This is it!" he called cheerfully as he whipped boxes out of the body of the plane. "The school's up there, it's not too far. Think you can manage?"

I was still clambering awkwardly out of the plane as he hauled the heavy dingy onto the dock and checked that nothing had been left behind. I nodded, trying to look more confident than I felt.

"Well that's it then. I'd best be off. Good luck!"

With a cheerful wave, the pilot untied the lines and swung back into his seat. The engine roared as the plane circled slowly around to face the mouth of the bay. Picking up speed, it was soon airborne, but I didn't bother to watch it disappear.

A man appeared on the deck of the closest floating house

and I waved to him, calling out, "Hello! I'm the new teacher!" He stared unsmiling for a few seconds then turned and disappeared inside. It didn't seem like an auspicious beginning. I wondered if all my neighbors were going to be as taciturn.

Turning to my boxes, I picked one and staggered up the ramp. It was low tide, and the ramp went up at such an angle that I couldn't have climbed it at all if not for rungs nailed across the boards. Despite the low tide, the bared beach was narrow. Shells and dead branches littered the stinking mud.

At the top, the vista was more promising. A grassy meadow with huge, well-groomed trees gave a park-like appearance. A charming path led to a small but prolific garden where a variety of vegetables and flowers grew, fenced against deer and hung with a shining array of tin lids to discourage birds. Obviously someone with an eye for beauty had been at work here, and it made me feel much more positive.

Setting down my box, I fetched up another one, and was panting most unbecomingly when a voice called out, "Hello!" Coming from the direction of the nearest float house was an apparition from the sixties. A tall, smiling woman with floating hair, beads, and ankle-length skirt was trailed by two little girls with wispy blond hair. She introduced herself as Rainbow Hurley, produced a key to the school, and offered to help me take the boxes up.

I was delighted to accept, especially as Rainbow knew where to find a wheelbarrow belonging to the school which made the job much easier. The children cavorted around us, as excited to meet the new teacher as I was to meet them. The elder girl, Summer Sunshine, told me that she would be in grade 3, and the only student able to walk to school. Autumn Mist, her sister, was four years younger and not in school yet.

The girls wore loose dresses, obviously homemade. With their long hair and delicate features they looked like small forest nymphs flitting about.

As we trudged with wheelbarrow and luggage through the meadow, I was eager for my first glimpse of the school. It wasn't long in coming. A chain-link fence marked the boundary between park and school yard. A lumpy and irregular field was sandwiched between the bay on our right, and a forbidding, forested hill that rose steeply on the left. A swing set and an ancient teeter totter faced each other across the shorn turf. At the far end of the field the school sat in the shade of the surrounding mountains and trees, a low building patched together from two white and green trimmed portables. Twin sets of stairs led to two brightly painted, orange doors.

"The school is on the left," Rainbow pointed out. "To the right, that's the teacherage. It's not in really good shape."

"I guess it will have to do, till Christmas at least," I replied. "Then my husband will come up with our boat. It's a twelve-meter trimaran. We'll live in that if the teacherage doesn't work out."

Rainbow nodded and pointed out a small shed almost hidden behind the school building. "That's your generator shed. The wheelbarrow goes in there. Sammy Potter will show you how to work the generator."

Rainbow used the key to unlock the door of the teacherage and I stepped inside. It was bright and reasonably clean looking, with only a hint of the musty smell that long-closed buildings develop.

"I came up here last week to clean and air the place," Rainbow explained as she hauled in a box. "I wanted it to be nice for you."

"Thank you so much!" I exclaimed, surprised and touched.

Eventually we had all of the boxes moved up to the teacherage, with the yellow dingy left tied upside down on the dock. Taking Summer Sunshine and Autumn Mist with her, Rainbow promised to look in on me the next day.

"Come down to the house if you want anything," she said. "It's easy to find, the first one you get to."

Much cheered by Rainbow's welcome, I took stock of what was to be my home for the next few months. A large window in the livingroom looked out over Blubber Bay, a view that compensated for much of the shabby drabness of the building. The walls were painted a discolored white, the floor of battleship grey tile, chipped and pocked. There was no furniture except for a formica table and a weathered grey couch, no carpeting and no curtains.

The kitchen had a small window too, looking over the school yard. A stove and fridge appeared to be in working condition, though without electricity nothing could be turned on. There was a single, enamel sink, chipped and scratched, and cupboards painted the same livid orange as the outside doors.

Behind the kitchen and livingroom there were two bedrooms, bare of everything except bedframes and mattresses, and a bathroom. The bathroom was windowless and so dark that I could hardly see a thing, but I was relieved to discover a washing machine and drier in there, as well as a tub.

The only other feature in the building was a large grate set in the middle of the floor. Peering down through it into the dusty and mysterious depths, I could only guess that it might cover a furnace. There was no other source of heat, and with the building positioned out of the sunlight, it was already growing cool.

I decided to push the table into the corner by the livingroom window. Presumably I could bring over chairs from the school room, and it would be a pleasant place to sit while I ate my meals and corrected papers. But no sooner had I shoved the table a short distance when one of the legs fell right through a hole in the floor! I hauled it out with some difficulty, as the leg was jammed right through the floor boards. It didn't surprise me to find that all four legs of the table were very loose and rickety; apparently they had been through this ordeal more than once before. Plugging the hole with a wad of paper to discourage mice and spiders, I got the table into the corner and turned to unpacking my boxes.

By this time the chill in the room was inescapable, and I had to use the toilet. I went through the boxes until I could find a flashlight, and approached the bathroom. Without power there was no running water, but when desperate . . . .

Rainbow had mentioned a neighbor who would show me how to work the generator. I wondered how to find him. But fortunately the second of my neighbors appeared just then, right on cue, an angel wearing denim and a tuque.

Chapter Two

Sammy Potter

It was not Sammy's style to knock at the door and introduce himself. Instead, he went directly to the generator shed and started it up, so that the first inkling I had of his presence was the unmuffled roar of an engine, accompanied by the bathroom light springing on. Startled, I hurried outside in time to see a solid, bashful man standing in the doorway of the generator shed, shaking his head sadly. He was wearing work clothes and a worn blue tuque that never left his head; I suspect he must have slept and bathed in that tuque as no one I knew ever saw him without it.

"Hello!" I called, hurrying over. "I'm Susan Todd. Are you Mr. Potter?"

"Sammy," he replied, wincing. "Everybody calls me Sammy." He was barely intelligible over the earsplitting racket behind him.

"Can you show me how to work the generator?"

"Wall, now," he sighed. "That's going to be a problem. This here generator, see, it's got a crank ignition. I don't think a woman could turn it."

A sexist misogynist, I thought, but I was wrong. Sammy wasn't prejudiced against women, he was merely stating a fact. I doubt if any woman short of an Olympic athlete could have turned that crank.

"Most teachers here have been men," Sammy explained. "Well, it can't be helped. I'll just have to come over and start the generator for you whenever you want the power on."

"Heavens, I can't ask you to do that," I protested. "There has to be another way."

"Wall, you could ask the School Board to install a push button ignition for you. It could be done, but how long it will take, I dunno."

"I'll ask them," I promised.

"Anything else I can help you with?" he asked.

"Well, it's pretty cold in the teacherage. Could you show me how to start the furnace?"

"Sure." Sammy led the way into the building and removed the grate from the floor. Kneeling beside the pit, he peered into the strange assemblage of dirt, metal and rust.

"God oh god oh god," he muttered. "It will be a miracle if this thing don't blow up."

"Is it dangerous?" I asked.

"Totally rusted out. I'll light it for you anyhow, but it's a real fire hazard." He fiddled with levers and knobs, dropping lit matches into the tank while I watched. "I wouldn't turn this off if I was you. It might not be so easy to get started again." Finally the furnace was creaking and humming, and sending out nauseating fumes of oil.

Sammy replaced the grating and stood up. "Want me to start the fridge and stove for you?"

"Won't they just plug in?"

"God no. They're propane. You won't want that generator running all the time. You'll probably just want it on in the evening, otherwise the noise will drive everyone crazy. Didn't you see the propane tanks out back?"

"No," I admitted. "I haven't had time to look around yet. I didn't know there were such things as propane fridges."

"Sure. You'll find it's a lot quieter than an electric fridge." He lay on the floor, removing a panel from the front of the appliance. See down here, here's where you light it. It's easy to do. You just turn on the propane and . . . . here we go! Just give it a couple of hours to get cold now."

The pilot lights in the stove were soon lit too, and the house was in order.

"The wife says you should come over for supper tomorrow night," Sammy said before he left. "About five o'clock would be good."

"Thanks! How do I get there?" I asked.

Sammy took me around behind the school. "See that trail?" he said, pointing to a barely perceptible path into the forest. "Follow that. Wear boots, because you'll have to walk over the mud flats, but it will be low tide. You can't miss it . . . . there's no where else to go."

He showed me how to turn off the generator when I was ready to go to bed, and I thanked him again. As Sammy disappeared among the trees, I turned back to survey the school more carefully.

The building had been painted fairly recently, with a lot of care. Green trim highlighted not only the doorframes and windows, but also neat window boxes that hung beneath the windows of the school. A tiny covered porch with three steps leading up to it stood in front of each door, with a home-made flag pole rising from above the school porch. The ceiling of the teacherage porch sagged ominously with rot.

Nothing grew in the window boxes except moss. I tried planting flowers each year I was there, but since the boxes never got any sun, and were constantly deluged by rain, every seed and bulb drowned before it could bloom.

Rainbow had left the school room unlocked, so I took my first look inside. I was pleasantly surprised to see a cheerful, well equipped, modern classroom. With an effort I forced myself back to my unpacking in the teacherage, saving the school room for dessert.

With the generator running, I was able to work far into the night. I was grateful that Richard had been able to keep Donna for the first few days, so that I could work without distractions. I discovered too, on this first night, that if I worked hard until long past midnight, and was up by six in the morning, I was far too exhausted to lie awake pining or to miss them too badly. I didn't have any trouble sticking to this schedule either, for the work needing to be done surpassed anything in my previous experience. But I hadn't discovered that yet.

Turning off the generator was an unexpectedly scary experience. Taking a flashlight with me I walked to the shed and pulled a small lever as Sammy had shown me. Immediately the whole area was plunged into total darkness, and a deadly silence. The flashlight gave only a feeble glow as I shut the shed door behind me and stood listening. The night sky was dark, the air was clear, and I'd hardly taken one step back toward the teacherage before I heard the sound of a large animal blundering about in the woods not a stone's throw away. Wolf? Bear? Cougar? Heart in my throat, but determined not to smell of fear, I walked briskly—but not hurrying—back to the welcoming porch, leapt through the doorway, and locked it behind me.

The following day I asked Sammy about the noise, and while he admitted that wolves, bears and cougars all lived on the island, he thought it was probably just a deer. "But the thing you got to look out for," he warned, "is the wild dogs. They got no fear of people. They run with the wolves, but wolves are afraid of people. Not dogs. Any time we see a wild dog around here, we shoot it." I hoped never to see a wild dog.

I worked hard the next day, and was soon comfortably moved in. Then it was time to set the school room in order. The only thing different from any conventional classroom of the time was the radio phone behind the teacher's desk. There was no telephone service this far from civilization, but the radio phone gave me a way to keep in touch with Frank Weston.

A modest library of novels and picture books filled one shelf, alongside dictionaries and a globe. The desks and furnishings were of good quality, and a well-stocked though disorganized book room held a wide selection of textbooks and Audio Visual equipment. Another small store room held gym equipment, deflated balls, easels, a floor waxer, almost a thousand rolls of toilet paper in boxes, custodial supplies, broken machinery, broken swings, pieces of lumber, flourescent tubes, drums of unidentified liquid contents, and a couple of shovels, all jammed in a tangled mess among the legs of several old desks and chairs. Apparently no one had tried to enter this room for some time.

Even to open the door was to risk life and limb. It looked like there was going to be enough work to keep me busy for some time.

Two low round tables, a large cupboard of games, and a comfortable carpeted area gave the room a cozy air. Large windows faced the schoolyard, and blackboards covered two of the walls. At the back of the classroom, the fourth wall was taken up by a small bulletin board, and doors to the storerooms and washroom.

A filing cabinet beside the teacher's desk drew my attention next. Hoping to find records on the students I would be teaching, I opened the top drawer. A wild array of unsorted papers gave me a shock of dismay. Was this a legacy of the disorganized Merv? The other drawers were the same. More work! At least I wasn't going to have much time for loneliness or boredom.

A battered brown piano tucked in one corner was the last treasure. I sat down and ran my hands over the keys. It was hideously out of tune, and some of the keys didn't play at all. Taking off the front panels, I looked inside. Broken strings, a cracked sounding board; it didn't look good. But it felt so fine to play a piano after years of doing without that I sat and played for some time, with my imagination filling in the notes that were missing.

Hunger drove me back to the teacherage for a late lunch, and a glance at the clock. I didn't want to be late for my supper at the Potters'. I warmed up a can of soup, then went outside to stroll around the school yard with an apple in my hand. A friendly brown rabbit lurked casually outside the door, obviously hoping for handouts, so I ate half the apple and gave him the rest. The rabbit, as I was later to learn, went by the name of Spud, and was very popular with the children at school. Most of the kids were popular with him too, and he would eat out of the quieter hands, though a couple of the younger boys had to be frequently reprimanded for chasing him.

Apple shared and rabbit patted, I went inside to sit at my rickety table and write the first of many long letters to Richard, while gazing out at the wonderful view of the bay. It was a harsh and magnificent beauty. Jagged slopes covered with impenetrable forest, choppy grey ocean beyond the mouth of the bay, and mountain heights that cut off the horizon inspired awe rather than comfort.

A little before five I put on my rubber boots and with a flashlight in my pocket for the homeward journey, I set off to find the Potter homestead. The faint path through the forest was easy to follow, and ended after a hundred meters or so at the narrow head of the bay. As Sammy had promised, the tide was low enough that I could walk across the short stretch of mud with ease. At the other side, trees had been felled to make a clearing. Two houses stood there, but one seemed to be under construction, so I headed for the more established looking dwelling.

Dogs barked as I stepped up onto the porch, and a woman's voice called out, "Teacher's here!" The door opened, and Sammy's face beamed from under his faded blue tuque.

"Come on in. Here, get away!" The first comment was to me, the second was addressed to two dogs who were eager to give their own greeting. Uncowed, the dogs walked off and lay down under a disused wood stove, keeping an eye on everything.

The interior of the house was dimly lighted but airy and open. Huge hand-hewn timbers supported the structure, which combined the best features of a Kwakiutl longhouse and a log cabin. Carved and painted Indian masks created by local artists hung about the walls.

Through a front window I could see a tiny bay on the far side of the house from Blubber Bay. A string of buildings on floats had recently been vacated by the Potters as they cleared their land and moved ashore. Pens and sheds housed many different varieties of animals, while cats and dogs wandered about freely. A long, open porch fronted the house.

Sammy's wife, known to everyone as Ma Potter, was a thin, energetic woman of about fifty. I initially took her for much older than she actually was, as Ma had made no effort to resist the aging that her rough lifestyle had imposed on her. Grey hair hung limply around a wrinkled but lively face and ulcerated legs made walking painful for her.

The third Potter was a daughter, recently married to a local forester. Emmy and Andy were building the other house that I had passed on my way from the mud flats. Besides Andy's work for a nearby logging company, the two of them kept busy managing a salmon hatchery in a nearby cove.

"Hey, Sammy, take Teacher up to see your museum, why don'cha, while I finish up supper," Ma suggested, and Sammy agreed with alacrity.

"Museum?" I asked.

"Oh, that's just Ma's joke. It's stuff I've collected from around here. Some people find it interesting."

Upstairs, a large room was lined with shelves. One wall was covered with books. The other shelves held a variety of artifacts, all neatly sorted.

"Have you read all these?" I asked, pausing to look at the titles.

"Oh, yeah. I didn't have but grade one education, but I learned how to read. Some of them I've read dozens of times." *Silas Marner, David Copperfield, Complete Works of William Shakespeare, The Rise and Fall of the Roman Empire, Pride and Prejudice, Moby Dick*—all the old classics were there. As time went by I would discover that Sammy had indeed read all these books, and pondered them, and extrapolated meaning from them. But the museum was what he wanted to show me now.

"What are these?" I asked, pausing at the first display.

"Opium bottles. The Chinese workers who were brought in at the turn of the century used a lot of opium. Their lives were mighty hard." The bottles were all small and of colored glass, but in a variety of shapes and colors.

"There's no railroad here. What were they doing?"

"There used to be a shingle mill up the hill behind the school. It's pretty hard to find where it was, now. Not much left but these bottles and a couple iron kettles all rusted out."

I took a lingering look at the cute little bottles. They were a reminder of sad lives that had indeed been harder than anything we nowadays could imagine.

"And these? They just look like ordinary pop bottles."

"Not just pop. Coke. Cocaine. The early homesteaders used Coca Cola for medicinal purposes. No wonder it made them feel better. You have to know where to look, but some of the old pioneer cabins had big piles of these bottles where they'd thrown them out the back door. Kept the pioneer ladies from going bonkers.

"These bottles are all hand-blown," Sammy continued. "See their thick bottoms? I like the colors of these. Yuh never see this pink shade any more."

"It must have been a lonely life" I said. "I've seen some of those rotted old cabins, a couple of hours' walk even from the nearest foot path. Nothing but rain forest all around; it would drive most people crazy."

"There was plenty who went that way. But those folks were tough. I'm minded of one fellow, Reb Jenkins by name, who lived in a bush shack all on his own years ago. There was no trail into his place, jest a bunch of felled trees you had to tightrope along to get to his place. Not so hard with cleats, but a different story with bare soles in the rain. Anyhow, he was packing in his cookstove, shipped up by a mail order company. Carried it on his back all that way, along those logs. And then he slipped and fell on his back, the weight of the stove holding him down. Couldn't get free and too proud to call for help. Figgered nobody would hear him. He'd of laid there till he died if somebody hadn't come by purely by good luck."

"Wow! There can't be that many chance wanderers strolling these woods. How about this, is this thing a fish hook?"

"Yeah, an old Indian halibut hook. Made of a sharpened twig steamed into a curve. And these are my arrowheads. Lots of 'em are from that shell beach over in Blubber Bay. There hasn't been an Indian village there since white men lived in these parts, but it was a summer village of theirs for hundreds of years. See this one, now that was a harpoon point. It was prob'ly made for seal. It's a real beauty, but see this one here? This was prob'ly a practice one. Anyhow, it was never used. You can see it warn't chipped right, and here the hammer slipped."

"Do you think I could find any arrowheads if I look?"

"Sure, if you keep your eyes open," Sammy said confidently, but in fact I never did find a single Indian artifact on that beach. Maybe he had found them all, but the truth is I think his eyes were just sharper than mine.

The beach reminded me, "Isn't that somebody's boat shed there? Who does that belong to?"

"That's mine," Sammy answered. "I haul my fishing boat up in there when I need to work on the bottom, but I don't know how much longer it'll be there. Martinette over at the store there, she thinks it's an eyesore. Afraid it'll turn off the American tourists."

"I haven't been over to the store yet," I said cautiously, remembering Frank Weston's warning about community quarrels. "But I thought your boat shed looked quite interesting there. You know, like part of the local culture."

"Yeah, well that's what I think, but Martinette, she sees it differently. I've lived here all my life, she moves in from a big city down south and thinks she can run the place."

I nodded non-committally and moved to the next shelf. "What's this stuff?" It looked like rusted junk from someone's storage shed.

"These are mainly logging and fishing tools from the turn of the century. Godalmighty, ain't supper ready yet? A man could wear out his stomach on his backbone before that woman gets dinner on the table."

Ma was a great cook who enjoyed watching people eat. From her scrawny frame I guessed that she didn't consume a lot herself, but everyone else certainly did justice to the meal. There was fresh baked fish, fresh bread, cooked vegetables, a jelly salad, two fruit pies and a Queen Elizabeth cake to choose from. Besides all that, several ornate jars of candy stood on shelves and tables around the room, from which the family helped themselves and encouraged guests to indulge when not actually in the act of eating a meal.

A fourth member of the Potter family had silently joined us as we sat down to eat. I wasn't sure whether the grim and awkward teenager was a boy or a girl. Lank black hair hung over the forehead and almost down to the hunched shoulders, and baggy overalls hid the shape of the body underneath.

"Don't mind Paddy," Ma laughed. "Paddy's a great hand with animals but not so good with people." Paddy didn't contribute a word, but that didn't stop anyone else from enjoying a raucous conversation. A large orange cat who had been dozing on a chair looked up with startled horror as he realized a stranger was sharing the meal, and he made as if to run for his life. Sam caught him up affectionately and spoke for the cat in a mock voice as he stroked the outraged animal.

"A stranger, oh my god what will I do? Call out the Mounties! Save me, save me!"

He put the cat down on the floor while Ma put a kettle to boil on their propane stove, and a moment later we heard her call out, "Sam, what're you doing to this poor cat? He just come running through here like a bat out of hell."

Sammy chuckled. "He's scared of the new teacher. Afraid she'll teach him something he don't want to know."

As we finished up our dessert, Paddy rose and tugged on gumboots, then slipped out the door. "Paddy!" Ma hollered. "I want you to take Granny her dinner." Paddy nodded and hovered on the porch while Ma loaded a plate and put it in a covered casserole dish. She handed it to Paddy then rejoined us at the table.

"Who's Granny?" I asked.

"My mother," Ma answered. "She lives in that last float house over there. She grew up in that house and has no mind to move onto land at this point in her life."

"Cantankerous old biddy," Sammy commented cheerfully.

"Cantankerous yourself," Ma retorted, and they both laughed.

Emmy told me later that Paddy was a girl, but that she would rather have been a boy. She had dropped out of school after grade seven, refusing to go on to high school as Emmy had done, since that involved boarding in Port McNeill. Most of the sheds and pens I had noticed were built to accommodate Paddy's menagerie of animals, which included rabbits, chinchillas, goats, and assorted fowl. She had hoped to add a horse to her collection, but there Sammy drew the line, and in fact it would have been a difficult climate and locality for a horse.

Emmy on the other hand was cosmopolitan and well educated. After finishing high school she had traveled before settling down with her boyfriend, Andy Morrison. Emmy and Andy were an exceptional couple, quiet and competent, liked by everyone, yet somehow able to stay apart from the omnipresent gossip.

I was sorry to leave when the evening was over. Gripping my flashlight, I made my way cautiously around the head of Blubber Bay. The tide had come up, and the unfamiliar terrain was confusing in the dark. I couldn't find the path, so blundered blindly through the trees with nothing to guide me. Finally, scratched and exhausted, I emerged from the woods behind the generator shed. But it had been worth it. I'd rarely had a more entertaining evening.

Chapter Three

Visitors

The next day I phoned Frank Weston at his school in Port Hardy.

"How are you getting along?" he asked.

"Fine. I've met Rainbow Hurley and Sammy Potter. But I can't start the generator by myself, it needs a push-button starter. And Sammy says the furnace is dangerous, it could blow up at any time. Can we get a maintenance man over here? And a piano tuner?"

"Well, I'll make a note of it," said Frank. He was as good as his word; a push-button starter was installed the following month, and a piano tuner did come over, though the furnace was never fixed.

"Frank, has there ever been a teacher who did get along in this community?" I asked.

"Certainly. There have been a couple. There was one, Mercy Goodman is her name, who lives there still. She ended up marrying a logger, and now she has a boy in school herself. You'll be meeting her, I'm sure."

"Why didn't Mercy want this job herself?" I wondered.

"I would guess she's probably too busy with her home and family. And I doubt they need the money; loggers make good pay."

"Do you know anything about the woman who runs the store?"

"Um, Martinette, Martinette Wilson I think her name is. She and her husband John run a resort over there for wealthy

American yachters. You won't see much of the tourists, though, not unless you decide to stay there all summer. It's the only store for fifty miles around so a lot of the north-bound yachts stop there. You'll be able to get some groceries there as well as your mail."

I noticed that Frank had evaded my question, but I let it go.

"How often does the mail come in?"

"Three times a week when the weather's good enough to fly." I was pleasantly surprised; that was better than some isolated communities I had lived in.

"School starts in four days. I'm going to need a teacher's aide until Richard gets here. Were you able to find someone?"

"Yes, Charlotte Hill has agreed to do it. She's one of the logging wives, has two kids in the school. She'll be coming over to meet you one of these days before school starts."

"Charlotte Hill," I repeated.

"Yes, she's a concerned parent, better spoken than some. I think you'll like her."

"I'm sure we'll get along fine. Okay then, I think we're all set."

"Let me know if you need anything."

"Right. Thanks Frank."

I had barely hung up the receiver when I heard a knock at the teacherage next door. Was it Rainbow? I hurried from behind the teacher's desk and to the door of the school.

A woman stood in the teacherage porch, nicely dressed and smiling.

"Hello!" I called.

"Hello. Are you the new teacher?"

"Yes, would you like to come in?"

Smiling she walked over and we seated ourselves at one of the small, round tables in the school room. *Another new neighbor*, I was thinking. *I wonder whose mother she is.*

Leaning forward earnestly, the woman looked intently into my face.

"Are you saved?" she asked.

"Uh, I beg your pardon?"

"Have you accepted our Lord Jesus Christ into your heart?"

"Um, I don't think so."

"The Lord Jehovah can save you and set you free."

"I'm sure he can," I replied. "Do you live around here?"

"No," the woman answered. "I live in Vancouver, but my husband and I spend our holiday each year bringing the Good Word to the godless people of the coast."

"Ohhh. How did you get here?"

"We have a boat, on loan to us from the mission," she said simply. "Have you read the Good Book?"

"Yes, several times," I retorted. "Well, I have to be getting back to work now. Nice to meet you."

"Let the Lord into your heart. He will hear your prayers. He knows your pain, He sees everything."

"Good. Then He sees that I'd better get back to work. Goodbye." I held the door open, and I doubted the smile on my face was a particularly pleasant one.

Sadly the lady got up. "Shall I leave you one of our magazines?"

"Sure, if you like. But your time might be better spent elsewhere."

I watched her trudge away through the chain-link boundary to my world, and wondered if I'd ever be lonely and desperate enough to welcome a visit from the Jehovah's Witnesses.

#

It was time for a bath. My unpacking and grubbing about had made me good and dirty, but I had been too charged up with excitement and adrenaline to take time for more than a sponge bath thus far. That evening as soon as Sammy had come over to turn on the generator, I started preparing for a luxurious soak. Towels, bath salts, soothing music on the tape deck . . . . hot steamy water in the tub. I turned the water on and waited.

The bathroom was a cozy room with an immensely high ceiling.

The electric washer and drier would only work when the generator was on, so I started a load of laundry while I prepared the bath. Black patches on the walls showed where bare wiring had scorched the paint, and brown drips festooned the walls, apparently from kerosene fumes. I tried scrubbing at them, but they wouldn't come off.

I'd already noticed that the toilet bowl was full of a brown slime which cast doubts on the previous tenants' housekeeping, but I soon learned that this was as permanent a feature as the brown drips on the wall. Our tap water, leached through cedar and the forest floor, was the colour of tea and stained everything. At first I was hesitant about bathing in it, doubting that such dark water could get anything clean, but eventually I learned to prefer the brown colour, much as some people prefer brown eggs to white. Clear city water eventually looked unwholesome and over-refined as we got used to the Blubber Bay run-off.

After repeated testing, I realized that the water was never going to get warm. In fact, thinking back, there hadn't been any hot water in the taps since I had moved in. I hadn't seen a hot water heater; was it possible there wasn't one? Or could it be propane and not turned on? Or perhaps electrical and given too few hours by the generator to heat a tank of water? I would have to ask Sammy when I saw him next.

In the meantime, I filled my biggest pots with water from the tap and put them on the stove to heat. It was a couple of hours before I could lower myself into a shallow, tepid bath; not at all the relaxing experience I'd been looking forward to.

The following day when Sammy arrived to start the generator, I asked about the hot water heater. I followed him to the equipment storeroom in the school, where he peered through the doorway at the tangled heap of desks, mops, boxes and canisters.

"God oh god oh god. I think it's in there somewhere. But we'll never get at it with all this stuff in the way."

"Do you know if it's electric?"

"I'm pretty sure. Maybe you better ask that principal of yours if he knows anything about it."

The next time I phoned Frank, I asked him about the hot water heater.

"What, hasn't that been fixed yet?" he exclaimed. "The last teacher put in a work order for that months ago. The Board office was supposed to have replaced it over the summer."

"Well I don't think they did."

"I'll make a note of it," Frank sighed.

#

On my fourth day in Blubber Bay I glanced up through the school window to see a huge woman toiling through the playground toward me. Her face was ruddy, her pale hair tied back in a pony-tail. A bright print dress covered her meaty form.

"Surely not another J.W.," I muttered as I went to the door and prepared to greet my visitor.

Panting, she smiled radiantly, and won me over in an instant. "I'm Charlotte Hill," she wheezed, holding out her hand. "Did Frank tell you about me?"

"Oh, yes, my teacher's aide. I'm so pleased to meet you! I hear you have a couple of children in the school."

"Yes, Veronica and Ricky. They wanted to come with me, but I told them they'd have to wait till Tuesday like everyone else."

Charlotte was an invaluable source of information. While she hadn't worked as an aide before, she had volunteered in the school. She knew where various blank forms were kept. She knew how the previous teacher had modified his program for a nine-year-old who could not read. She knew all the people in the community, and had plenty to say about each one.

And what's more, she had her own little motor boat. "Is that yellow rowboat yours?" she asked. "That's fine for getting across to the store for your mail, but it's useless for going anywhere else. If you want to go somewhere, you ask me and I'll take you."

Charlotte went over the class list with me and confirmed the grade levels of my students. I'd already done a lot of lesson preparation, so we were able to work out our different responsibilities and routines very easily. Charlotte would tutor individuals and small groups throughout the day while I planned all the lessons and taught the curriculum.

As my hefty aide waddled away, I felt very positive about the coming school year. Charlotte was clearly an energetic and positive person with a pleasant personality. I certainly hadn't seen anyone from the community so far who posed the kind of threat that Frank had warned me about.

With Charlotte's help, I had a good day's work finished in my classroom, and plenty of daylight left. I grabbed my wallet from the teacherage and headed down to the jetty for a trip to the local store.

Flipping my heavy dingy into the water, I looked across the bay. Three large cabin cruisers were tied up at the resort dock, where people could be seen walking about and talking to each other. My trip across the water took less than ten minutes. For the most part I rowed backwards so I could see where I was going.

A gas pump in a floating shed did a steady business with small local boats that motored in. Up the hill in the large building that I had seen on my first day, well heeled tourists sat on a deck. I could imagine the fancy drinks beside them.

A small, trailer-like building to the left of the docks advertised *Ice and Bait*. I tied up my boat nearby and looked inside. It was a small general store, not well stocked, but with a steady clientele. Tourists and locals hung around making small talk. A small, loud man in a faded shirt was boasting, "Those Hindus, we don't want them here, them with their diapers on their heads, and taking jobs from folks who grew up in this great land of ours."

I stared in distaste while another man grunted agreement through the cigarette held in his teeth. He hawked and made as if to spit, but suddenly a woman's voice cut through their talk.

"Don't you spit in here! Go out on the dock for that."

The hawking man rolled his eyes but obliged, stepping outside and clearing his throat loudly as he spat into the water. I hoped that it had landed well clear of my dingy.

I looked at the woman, clearly the proprietor of the store. Severe and gimlet faced, she eyed me.

"You off a boat? I've never seen you before."

"I'm the new teacher," I said.

"The new school marm!" laughed the small, loud man. "School marms all the same, tight in the . . ." His comment withered as the woman stared at him frostily.

"I'm Martinette Wilson."

"How do you do. Do I pick up my mail here?"

"Yes, right over here. In fact, I've got a couple of things waiting for you."

She rummaged behind a counter and produced two envelopes. One was from Richard, I was pleased to see; the other from the School Board.

"Thanks. Is it okay if I look around?"

"Go ahead," Martinette smiled. I tried to look at the displays while avoiding the gossiping men, but I couldn't help overhearing their conversation. I wondered if I should speak up, but decided not to. Sometimes the coward's way is wiser.

There were a lot of canned goods in the store, priced about three times as high as those I had brought up with me from Victoria. In a cooler, beer, pop and cartons of milk were ranged. The beer and pop didn't interest me, but we were all big milk drinkers in my family. A one liter box of milk cost $3.62. The two liter boxes were $5.84, an exorbitant price in 1982. The dates stamped on the tops of the cartons had all expired.

Martinette was watching me. "It comes up on a barge from Vancouver," she explained, "the milk and the produce. It often takes two weeks to get here. It's expired before I even receive it in the store."

"Does anyone buy it?" I asked.

"Oh yes, it all sells."

But not to me, I decided.

The produce was no better. Withered and spotty, it looked inedible. I'd have to ask Richard to bring up plenty of canned and dried fruit and vegetables when he moved up with us. Not to mention milk powder.

It was a relief to get back into my boat and row away from there. I felt like I was speeding from a den of filth back to the sunshine and clean air on my own side of the bay.

As I docked, Rainbow came out of her house and waved. "Hello! Would you like a cup of tea?"

"I'd love one," I called back. After hauling my boat up onto the dock and securing it, I climbed the ramp and made my way down toward Rainbow's house. Two huge logs were coupled side by side and covered with a plank walkway. I balanced cautiously along it, while the two little girls hopped up and down at the far end.

"Mrs. Todd, Mrs. Todd! Would you like to see our room? Look at my dress!" They twirled and bounced as gracefully as butterflies. Rainbow appeared, laughing.

"Girls, let the teacher come inside. They're so excited," she apologized.

"They're lovely. Yes, I'd love to see your room," I answered as they each took one of my hands. The girls showed me around their house while their mother made the tea. It was a unique and charming home, built by Rainbow's husband Geoff, and decorated by Rainbow herself. A huge round bubble window dominated the livingroom, which was hung with tapestries and beadwork. Benches covered with rugs and pillows took the place of more conventional furniture.

Once Summer Sunshine and Autumn Mist had given me the tour, we settled around the kitchen table. The children had mugs of tea too.

"Mmm, mint," I breathed.

"I grow it in my garden at the top of the hill," Rainbow smiled.

"Try one of Mom's cookies," Summer Sunshine offered. "They're our favorite!"

"Molasses snaps," said Rainbow, passing the plate.

"This is so nice," I exclaimed. "I was over at the store this afternoon."

Rainbow's face sobered. "We have to keep on good terms with them to get our mail, but it isn't easy."

"How do you mean?"

"Families like us. We're here because we've turned our backs on cities, on civilization. We don't want T.V., we don't want pollution. We want to bring up our children simply, to appreciate nature."

"Don't the Wilsons do that?"

"John maybe. He's a nice enough guy. But those power boats with their big engines, their lights, their loud music. They're the kind of people Martinette caters to. They don't care about the Earth. Geoff has complained a few times, when they play the music too loud all night, or when speed boats blast around in the bay, but it does no good."

"Sammy Potter said he had some trouble with Martinette too," I remembered.

Rainbow nodded. "His boat house. It's been there for as long as anyone can remember, but Martinette wants to get rid of it. She says it's not scenic enough."

I shook my head, thinking of Frank's words. *Don't get drawn in, don't take sides. Until they step onto school property it's not the teacher's business what they choose to fight about.* It appeared that would be easier said than done. I knew which side I was on already.

Chapter Four

School

The next day Donna arrived on the same plane that had brought me four days earlier. What a four days it had been! I felt as if I had stepped into a whole new world, a new planet almost.

When I heard the plane taxiing in toward our jetty I dropped everything and ran as fast as I could. Again the pilot drifted up to the dock perfectly, stepping off the pontoon with his mooring line. Donna's face behind the window looked excited and anxious.

It felt so good to hug each other again! But our reunion would have to wait until the plane was unloaded and boxes hauled up the ramp. Donna's luggage was easier to handle than mine had been, since I'd already brought our food and household supplies. As well as her clothing and toys, Richard had sent along a few more boxes of books, and a carton of treats from my mother.

The carton, when unpacked, yielded a gold mine of treasures. Curtains for the bare windows—not really needed, given our lack of neighbors, but they'd make the place so much more homey. Homemade baking and a plastic container of cut up vegetables. A hummingbird feeder, Hallowe'en make-up, health food snacks, hobby kits—it was better than Christmas. During our years in Blubber Bay, my mother was to meet requests for items stranger than these, and she never let me down.

Donna and I spent an enjoyable day catching up on news and moving her stuff into the smaller of the two bedrooms. She was thrilled with everything, especially having the school room right next door. Never having been keen on walking to school, this was a set-up that suited her perfectly.

The following day was the last one before school was to open. On Labor Day we rested, and Donna became good friends with Summer Sunshine despite the two-year difference in their ages. I took her to visit the Potters too, and with Ma's kind insistence that Donna sample all their candy jars, Donna was convinced that they were the best of all possible neighbors.

With a child to keep clean, the broken water heater became a more urgent problem. I took to phoning Frank almost daily in the two months that followed. Donna and I tried bathing from every conceivable bucket and basin as well as the kitchen sink; we tried heating water in every pan and kettle to fill the tub, but nothing really did the trick. It was a happy day when the School Board sent over a maintenance crew to install a new hot water heater at last.

By then I'd had a chance to clear out the school store room, and to throw away the broken items that added to the clutter. Shovels and lumber were tucked into the generator shed and the thousand rolls of toilet paper found a new home on top of a hard-to-reach cupboard.

#

On the first day of school, we were up and ready early. I don't know who was more excited, Donna or the new teacher. We watched through the school room windows for our students to arrive.

The first to march over the hill was Charlotte Hill, with Veronica and Ricky in tow. Veronica looked to be about Donna's age; Ricky had his mother's freckles and red coloring, and was a couple of years younger than his sister.

A minute or two later a large group of children arrived en

masse. Counting rapidly, it looked like eight boys and girls. Summer Sunshine came running through the gap in the fence behind them.

"Those are the children from Pierre's school boat," gasped Charlotte as she came through the door and nodded cheerfully at Donna. I smiled at her two children and said "Hello," but they stared back with sullen expressions. *Perhaps just shy?* I wondered.

More children were arriving. "Mercy Goodman's boy," Charlotte said. "And Helen and Stephanie Potts. They drive themselves."

The children crowded into the classroom, and I seated them on the rug. "Let's get to know one another," I suggested. "Who are we missing?"

"Danny Storto," said Veronica. "He won't come till the truant officer makes him."

"Veronica!" Charlotte hushed, though with a look of fond pride. "The children from the Indian reservation are missing too. They'll probably be here later."

"Then we'll get started without them."

We went through the activities and routines I had planned without any problems. The children seemed cheerful and willing, for the most part. There were some curious combinations, though.

Three children from the Campbell family were in grade four, with another sister in grade five and the youngest brother in kindergarten. Charlotte explained at recess time that the five children were a blended family, the two boys products of their father's first marriage, while the three girls were from their mother's first marriage. The two sisters in grade four were twins.

While we watched the students race around outside during their break, I had a good opportunity to ask Charlotte for more information about my students.

"Those two sisters, the ones you said drove themselves. What did you mean?"

"Their family had a big fight with Pierre last year. They won't go on the school boat. Their father bought them their own speed boat, and Stephanie drives it to school."

"She's the younger one?"

"Yes, but she gets her way in everything."

I could see why. Ten-year-old Stephanie looked confident, sexually precocious, and very attractive. Her older sister Helen was fat, pasty, and dull looking. I'd only heard her speak in a low mumble.

"And that pretty girl?"

"Patsy Edenshaw. Her family lives in a float house not far from here. Her father's a fisherman. They're Kwakiutl, a very fine family. You'll have no trouble with her."

Wilson Goodman was the nine-year-old who could not read. He was a big boy, but with an earnest innocence on his face. He ran around with the other children, not really understanding the rules of their game, but having a great time.

As I reluctantly rang the hand bell to call the children inside, we were surprised by four more children traipsing over the hill from the jetty.

"The kids from the reservation," Charlotte murmured. "They're all here."

"Do they always come this late?"

"No, not always. It's unpredictable."

Our students went back inside, and those who had been there all along took their seats and resumed work under Charlotte's eye. I paused on the steps to greet our four newcomers. Three boys and a slim girl came toward me, straight black hair and resigned faces giving them a look of solidarity.

"Hi," I smiled. "I'm the new teacher, Mrs. Todd. You must be the Davidsons."

The girl and the biggest boy smiled and said "Hello." The youngest boy, Jason, did more than that. With a flying leap, he landed beside me on the stairs and gave me a big hug. Only the middle boy, Timothy, hung back.

"Come on in, I've got desks ready for you," I invited. We went inside and I fetched assignments for the children. Angelica looked at hers, then spent her time rotating in her seat while she tried to see what everyone else was doing. The oldest boy, Patrick, tried hard to do his work, but he was clearly frustrated by it.

"Miss, I need help," he kept saying, but he did seem sincerely to be doing his best.

Timothy refused to sit in his desk. He climbed on top of a table and stood there like an animal at bay. When I tried to persuade him to come down, he leapt wildly off and on several pieces of furniture, while the other children screamed in mock terror. Finally I decided to leave him where he was, so long as he wasn't disrupting anyone else.

And sweet Jason giggled uncontrollably. He didn't get any work done either, but he was certainly cheerful about it.

Lunchtime couldn't come too soon. We all ate at our desks, then again the children went outside to play while Charlotte and I watched.

"It's a good thing there are two of us," I observed, "or we'd never get a chance to go to the washroom or have any break at all."

"That's true," Charlotte agreed.

"The Davidson children. Tell me about them."

"They're good kids, really they are. You'll see. They're smart too. They moved here last year from Alert Bay. They've had some real problems in that family. The mom used to drink, but I think she stopped when they moved to the reservation here. There was a little sister who died, I don't know how. And a couple of years ago in Alert Bay, Timmy was set on by some older children. They tried to force him to sniff glue, and when he refused they doused his legs with gasoline and set him on fire. He ran home, but his mother was out drinking. Patrick loaded his brother onto a bicycle and rode him to the hospital."

"My god!" I exclaimed, horrified.

"It makes you think, doesn't it. Patrick is really the one who looks after the other two boys. Their mom, I guess she tries, I don't know. Angelica is their cousin, not their sister."

I didn't know what to say. Suddenly Timothy's behavior seemed easier to understand.

"Timothy needs an operation on his legs," Charlotte continued. "The scars don't grow with the rest of him. He needs to go to the hospital in Alert Bay for skin grafts, but his mother hasn't taken him."

"Can't we do anything?"

Charlotte shrugged. "You can try."

Mentally reeling, I looked at the other children on the field. Most of them played a good-natured game of soccer baseball. Others hung around the swing set, waiting for turns. Timothy stood alone, glowering as he kicked at the ground.

"Who's that one?" I pointed at a small, good-looking boy who appeared to be a gifted athlete.

"Sylvain Lemieux, Pierre's son. Now there's a well adjusted boy. Very smart, too. And that other boy, that's Hans Baker, another good student."

"Thank goodness." After hearing Timothy's sad story, I needed some positive news.

The afternoon went better, now that I had the necessary background on my students. We had gym class outside, then the children drew pictures of their families with descriptive paragraphs beneath. Timothy refused to draw a picture of his family.

At the end of the day, I walked my flock to the waterfront to meet their boats. Pierre was there in his big school boat. He roared a greeting as we scrambled down the ramp.

Sylvain grinned at his father, hopping aboard. They talked cheerfully while the Campbell children, Patsy Edenshaw, and Hans joined them. Pierre supervised as the children all strapped on their life jackets, then with much waving and calling, they were off.

Stephanie and Helen climbed into their small run-about. Stephanie took the wheel while Charlotte cast off for her.

A motorboat driven by a grim-faced Indian man drove up, and the four Davidson children got in. Patrick, Angelica, and Jason waved good-bye. Timothy and the adult ignored us.

Charlotte, Veronica and Ricky climbed into their boat and put on life jackets while I held their lines. Soon only Donna, Summer Sunshine, and Wilson Goodman were left with me on the dock.

"Wilson, who do you go home with?" I asked.

"My grandma. She comes every day to clean the school, then I go home with her."

"Oh, that's nice! Your grandma is our janitor, and your mom used to teach school here."

"Yes," Wilson grinned. "And I have a little brother, Bobby, and he's going to come to school here next year."

"So is my sister," said Summer Sunshine. "They'll both be in kindergarten."

The three kids ran off to play together, while I returned to my classroom to tidy up and prepare for the next day.

Wilson's grandma arrived soon after. Sylvia Goodman was an aging but attractive woman, slim, energetic, and bright. She was unusually well groomed and tastefully dressed for that area, as most people didn't seem to think it was worth the bother. I soon began looking forward to seeing Sylvia at the end of each day, since like Charlotte she was a cheerful and hard-working font of information.

Chapter Five

Pierre

As time went by, I got to know more of my neighbors. One of the most admirable was Pierre Lemieux, the school boat driver. I remembered that Frank had mentioned that the previous teacher had become involved in a fight over the school boat, and I was curious to know what had happened. Rainbow and Charlotte soon filled me in.

The problem had started when Pierre decided that in order to run the boat safely, his charges should sit in one spot, wear life jackets, and avoid excessive fighting. These rules did not go over well with those of the children who enjoyed fighting or were used to having their own way. Further problems developed when Stephanie Potts began deliberately to keep the boat waiting for her, and the situation escalated into open defiance.

Pierre, a mild and gentle man, soon found himself ferrying a venomous zoo, with the few students who were not involved in the viciousness and disobedience feeling as disturbed by it as he was. Pierre tried talking to the parents about what was happening, but was roundly criticized for "trying to tell them how to bring up their children." The situation finally came to a head when Pierre asked to see something that Ricky Hill was holding, and Ricky spat in his face. Charlotte took Ricky's part although she did not condone the spitting, and a public meeting

47

was held with School Board members and the district superintendent to discuss the problem.

Stephanie's parents said that they were planning to buy her a speedboat of her own anyway, and they had no need of a school boat. Charlotte said that children should have a right to privacy, and that Pierre was too controlling. The Campbells said that they preferred to drive their children themselves. And that was that. Pierre was soundly vilified, insulted, and left without a job. The one cry for moderation came from Patsy Edenshaw's mother, who protested that it was the middle of winter, and that everyone was bushed in and suffering from "cabin fever." Her protests did not have much effect on the final outcome of the meeting, however.

It wasn't long before the Campbells grew tired of driving their large brood to school every day, and soon the children were admitting that they liked Pierre and they had treated him unfairly. They agreed that they had been rude and unreasonable, so Pierre said that he would start the route again, driving his own son Sylvain, the Campbell children, Patsy Edenshaw, and Hans Baker. He ferried Danny Storto too, on the rare day that the boy made it to school.

I noticed that Stephanie failed to tie up her speedboat properly on several occasions, and more than once Pierre saved the boat from drifting away. He also had to get the engine going for her more than once. Stephanie and Helen arrived late for school more often than not, and eventually stopped attending school more than two or three days a week. They both dropped out of school after grade eight.

The Campbells didn't really need the transportation allowance that was Pierre's only source of income, since Mr. Campbell was a logging foreman. I was relieved that they had decided to let Pierre have his job back, since without Pierre I couldn't be certain of having more than five or six of my students turn up on time. It was hard planning lessons for children who frequently turned up late or not at all.

Throughout these difficult months, Pierre came to school many lunch hours to play ball with the kids. Out of work and heavily in debt, he continued to be pleasant and helpful to all the people who had wronged him, and he and his wife refused to speak ill of anyone or to carry a grudge. Finally Pierre was able to get a job in the logging camp. He was an artist and a well educated man, but he was willing to work at heavy labor for the pay cheque his family needed.

#

Blubber Bay was not only a conservative community, it was a Christian community. Pierre Lemieux and his wife Denise were Christians, and to me they were the real thing. Prayer, love, and forgiveness were as familiar to them as breathing and sleeping. They brought up their children strictly and with high expectations, but with love and reverence for their God.

Virtually everyone else called themselves Christians too, especially those who had encouraged their children in defiance, or who had lied or helped Pierre out of his school boat job.

Soon these people began to cast a suspicious eye on me, for I do *not* call myself a Christian. So I began to wonder, if they could treat Pierre, who was one of their own, with such callous and deceitful cruelty, what might they do to me, an unbeliever?

With this in mind, I was glad to start attending Pierre's monthly prayer services, not only to cover my backside from vicious gossip, but also because I sincerely enjoyed the company. "Church" in Blubber Bay was run by a Pentecostal missionary and his wife who worked out of Alert Bay, traveling by boat around a small circuit of tiny communities. Once a month they would hold a service either at Pierre and Denise's float house, or in the home of our school custodian, Sylvia Goodman. The service consisted of a great many hymns, prayer, a short and simple sermon, and then a potluck lunch. They were small and pleasant gatherings, attended by the Lemieux family and the Goodmans, but rarely by anyone else.

It felt odd to be ministered to by itinerant preachers. When I had lived in the city and met such people I thought of them as missionaries who visited lonely, isolated folks way "up north." Now that meant me. I could remember as a child collecting Christmas parcels for the missionaries to distribute to poor souls who never saw a department store Santa; now we were on the receiving end.

Pastor Clive Smith and his wife Marjorie were just a couple of years from retirement when I first met them. They had met in Bible college and spent the whole forty years of their married life in boat ministries, first in Alaska, then Bella Coola, and finally the north of Vancouver Island. They were a humble and hard-working couple, always pleasant and willing to lend a helping hand. Despite a limited income Pastor Smith always appeared dapper and well dressed, but he was always ready to tie up a boat, fix an engine, or do whatever else needed doing, neatly pressed suit notwithstanding.

Pastor Smith and his wife spoke in tongues and believed in the laying on of hands. At one monthly service I had a persistent headache that had dogged me for days. Noticing that I wasn't my usual self, Pastor Smith insisted on knowing the reason why. I was embarrassed when he laid his hands on my head and said a short prayer, but amazingly enough my headache cleared up instantly. I was humbled to discover that God's miracles work even on unbelievers.

The best part of our monthly prayer services were the potluck dinners. The food was plentiful, and the company was jolly. A favorite with everyone was Sylvia's husband George. A big man, he was missing three fingers on his right hand. They had been cut off by a fishing line when he was a boy.

George was a great story teller. He loved to talk about his mother. During a visit to Vancouver in her youth, she had been standing in the street, listening to a Salvation Army band when one of the uniformed ladies asked her if she had found Jesus.

"Hell, no!" she replied. "Is he lost?"

On another occasion, on a hunting trip with her husband, the tide was out and he was struggling to haul their boat over long mud flats. After watching him sweat and heave for a while,

George's mother groped in her pockets. "Never mind," she said. "Here's a streetcar ticket!"

Although the food was always good at our potlucks, some concoctions were not to everyone's taste. George's eyes went wide at one Sunday gathering as he tasted a punch made of pear juice and freshie. "Jesus, what is this stuff?!" he roared. "Give me something to get the taste out. An apple, that'll do."

As he munched it down, Pastor Smith observed, "An apple a day keeps the doctor away. An onion a day keeps *everyone* away. And as for garlic—give it a week!"

George roared with laughter while Sylvia observed, "We love watching George laugh. There's so much of him to be jolly!"

George was not a religious man, and he often dozed off during Pastor Smith's sermons. Once, as his head dropped forward and he started snoring loudly, Sylvia spoke up.

"Well, as the horse trader said when his horse fell over dead, I never saw him do that before!"

Not easily offended, Pastor Smith's wife looked fondly at the snoring man. "Well, isn't that cute."

George snorted awake and looked around. "Is the sermon finished? Why's everyone staring at me? I suppose you're all waiting for a story.

"Okay then, here's one. There was this old feller, a bachelor all his life, but getting on in years. He was a well-liked old codger with lots of friends and a pretty well heeled bank book, but no kids to leave the shebang to. So, somebody tells him one day about these sperm banks, and he decides to go see if they'll take him, old as he is, and at least he'll have offspring that way.

"Well, he talks to the receptionist and she gives him a jar. Go into that little room, she says, so off he goes. Time goes by. He's in there all day! But they think, well he's pretty old. Finally it's quitting time and they're getting worried. They're knocking on the door.

"The old guy comes out and looks around pitifully. *I tried it with my right hand, he says, then I tried with my left hand, then I tried with both hands. I tried running it under hot water, and I ran it under cold water. But I never did get the lid off that jar.*"

George laughed louder than anybody at his own jokes.

"George," Sylvia said reproachfully. "Pastor Smith was right in the middle of his sermon."

But even if George's stories did sometimes stretch the bounds of good taste, Mercy Goodman could always be counted on to giggle, "Isn't that *funny*?!"

Chapter Six

Parents

One evening soon after the beginning of the school year, Donna and I were startled by a knock on the door. A young man stood on the teacherage porch, holding a large fish with his fingers hooked through its gills.

"I've brought you a house warming present," he said, smiling.

I accepted the fish gingerly though with sincere thanks, and put it on a baking sheet in the fridge. Being unversed in local fish etiquette, I was unsure whether I should offer to cook it immediately and invite our visitor to eat with us. Who was he?

"We've already had our supper, but it will be wonderful tomorrow night. Are you the father of one of my students?" He looked too young to be anyone's father. Donna and I sat side by side on the grey couch and looked at him expectantly.

"Not exactly."

The young man looked around the walls of the teacherage.

"I see you like to read. You've fixed the place up a bit."

I nodded. Surely he couldn't be another Jehovah's Witness. Should I demand to know his name?

"I'm Susan Todd," I said finally. "This is Donna."

"I know."

We continued to sit in silence.

"Are you a neighbor?" I asked.

"Sort of."

Donna wriggled impatiently then demanded, "Who *are* you? Where do you live?"

The young man looked surprised. "My name is Rod McFarlane. I live in Abalone Bay, a couple of miles west of here."

Now it started to make sense. Sylvia and George Goodman had pointed out Abalone Bay to us the week before, while on our way to Pierre's monthly prayer meeting. The Goodmans had picked up Donna and me in their power boat and pointed out local landmarks on the way.

"You live near Pierre and Denise Lemieux then. Are you Hans Baker's father?" Hans was a fine looking and intelligent boy in grade 5, the same age as Donna.

"No, not his father. I live with Giselle, Hans's mother."

"Oh. You're his stepfather then."

"In a way."

There was another long pause.

"Will Giselle be coming to meet me?" I asked. "I like to meet the parents of all my students."

Rod stared up at the ceiling and studied it for a while. "I don't know. She doesn't go out much."

"She must be shy."

"No, not shy." Rod leaned forward and spoke confidentially. "She just doesn't like people much. When she moved here from Vancouver she said that she'd had enough of people to last her a lifetime. But I like to get out and visit."

"Well you're welcome any time," I said, hoping that he wouldn't take me literally.

Rod smiled. "Maybe I can get Giselle to come. Hans talks about you all the time."

"He's a fine boy. It's good luck for Hans that you live so close to the Lemieux's. He and Sylvain must be good friends."

Rod got up to leave. "No, not really. Giselle doesn't believe in imposing on neighbors."

"Imposing? But you live in adjoining bays. Surely the boys must want to play."

"Goodbye," said Rod. "It's been real nice to meet you."

Donna and I looked at each other in bafflement as Rod walked away down the field. It had been a strange visit. I'd have to ask Charlotte what she knew about Giselle Baker.

#

Although Charlotte was a good teacher's aide, she was a mother first. I noticed it when I learned how she defended her son Ricky after the spitting incident in the school boat. And I noticed it every day thereafter.

Ricky was not a well-behaved boy. A lazy and self-satisfied eight-year-old, he preferred to rock in his chair rather than do his school work. Since Ricky was a non-reader, and Charlotte was assigned to work with him and Wilson Goodman for much of the day, this presented a problem.

Fortunately Veronica was a good student, but she could be proud and wilful. She resented Donna, so my hope that the two girls would become friends didn't last long. But I hoped that Charlotte and I could remain friends.

Unfortunately she couldn't tell me much about Hans Baker's mother.

"Nobody really knows Giselle," Charlotte said when I asked her. "They moved up from Vancouver almost a year ago, and Rod moved in with them soon after. He'd been around these parts for quite a while, so I don't know how they got to know each other.

"Hans is a nice boy, but his mother is a bit strange. Reclusive, you know? She doesn't seem to welcome visitors. I stopped by to see her once, but she just shouted from the doorway that she didn't want any company. It must be hard on the boy."

"Hans seems so well adjusted," I said.

"Yes, but there are things . . ."

"What kinds of things?"

"Did you know he still sleeps with his mother?"

"What? But what about Rod? I thought they . . ."

Charlotte shrugged. "That's as may be. But the boy does sleep with his mother. Ask him, he makes no secret of it. I don't think he even knows it's unusual."

#

It wasn't easy to slip an inquiry about Hans's sleeping arrangements into casual conversation with the boy. Time went by and I almost forgot about it. Once I asked Pierre what he knew about the family, but since Pierre was never one to gossip I didn't learn anything that I didn't already know.

In the meantime, Ricky Hill was growing more defiant and indolent. While Wilson sweated over his early reader books, Ricky would rock and grin, kicking at the legs of the table where they worked. Since Charlotte never scolded or disciplined him, one day when the class was working well I attempted to talk to Ricky about his attitude. Ricky grinned and rocked while I tried to get him to sit still and make eye contact.

Finally I realized that rather than continuing to work with Wilson, Charlotte was sitting and glowering at me. Clearly Ricky had no intention of listening at all, while Charlotte was ready to spring to the defense of her cub. I gave it up for that day. However, only a couple of days later when Charlotte called on the boys to come and read with her, Ricky deliberately ignored her and carried on with the picture he was scribbling on the top of his desk.

"Come on, Ricky honey," Charlotte wheedled, while I looked daggers at her son. When Ricky didn't respond, I got up and lifted him out of his desk by the armpits. Frog-marching him over to Charlotte's table, I said, "When your mother calls you, you listen!"

Ricky sat in his chair, unmoved. But Charlotte's eyes held fury and a promise that this was something she wouldn't forget.

#

Ricky and his mother were not my only challenge. Timothy Davidson continued to be a worry. He no longer leapt from desk to desk like a frightened animal, but he rarely talked and he never did any school work. His older brother Patrick told me that Timmy was often in pain, but it seemed to me that his emotional trauma had to be worse than any physical scars.

The Campbell children were a handful too, or at least the girls were. Garth Campbell, in grade 4, and his little brother Davy were stalwart and reliable boys, and good students. Garth and Sylvain Lemieux were best friends; I was glad for their sake that the school boat fiasco had blown over.

However, Lisa Campbell and her twin sisters, Laverne and Lindsay, were another matter. Lisa was a pretty child, but clingy. Whenever she could, she would sit beside Charlotte or me, stroking our arms or holding a hand. She often begged to stay in with us at recess, or to help out with special jobs. Lisa could pout and was often given to sulks, especially when her sisters were getting attention, but she felt an almost desperate need to please and for approval.

The twins, on the other hand, were brassy and confident. With identical chunky physiques and tight curly hair, they bulldozed through school life in noisy concert, often getting their way through the force of sheer numbers. They didn't take learning seriously, but they managed to do enough work to keep out of trouble.

#

I was pleased when Mrs. Campbell came for a visit mid-way through September. I recognized her immediately, a middle-aged version of her twin girls.

She huffed and puffed her way into the classroom one afternoon after my students had gone home, almost as stout as Charlotte but a good deal less fit.

"I come over in Stephanie's boat to meet the new teacher," she announced. "That you? I told Mrs. Potts she oughta come with me, meet the new teacher I said. But she wouldn't come. I told her you gotta take an interest in your kids' education. But she don't pay no nevermind.

"How's my kids doing? You gotta keep a firm hand with 'em you know. You don't want to let 'em run wild. That Merv there, he didn't know nothin' about keeping discipline. You got any experience?"

"Yes, quite a bit," I broke in. "I'm so pleased you've come. I'd like to speak with you about Lisa . . ."

"Now Merv there, I told him. I told him don't you let those kids get the upper hand. They need to be told who's boss.

"There's a lot of us think Mercy should be the teacher. I don't know why that principal in Port Hardy wants to hire strangers from down south when we've got a perfectly good teacher up here."

"I agree," I answered, "but Mercy didn't apply. I don't think she wants the job."

"Of course she wants the job. And I've told my kids, if Mercy was their teacher I wouldn't stand for no misbehavior. No, they would obey their teacher! And nobody ever lays a hand on my kids, nobody but me, but if Mercy was their teacher she could give them a licking. I would know they deserved it if Mercy lit into them."

"Let me see if I've got this right," I said. "You want me to keep discipline, but if Mercy was the teacher, you would let her hit your kids."

"Damn right. Because Mercy's a good teacher."

"Has she ever taught any of your children?"

"Of course not. My Lisa was just a little baby when Mercy was teacher here."

"Then how do you know she's a good teacher?" I knew I was treading on thin ice, but my curiosity and sense of the outrageous had got the better of me.

"Of course she's a good teacher. She's a Goodman." Mrs. Campbell puffed to her feet. "We'll see how long you last. You all on your own here?"

"My husband will be coming up at Christmas," I said. "Donna's father, you know."

"Mercy's husband is a logger, a local feller. Mercy knows all the kids here 'bouts. You'll find a lot of folks prefer those they know."

If Mercy was such a good teacher, I wished she would teach poor Wilson to read. He wanted so badly to know what the words in books said, and he would sit by the hour while Charlotte or Sylvain Lemieux read aloud to him. But no one except Sylvia ever read to the boy at home.

#

Shortly before the Christmas holidays Sylvia Goodman told me that she and George were "going out" for a few days. They would be shopping and visiting with friends in Campbell River. In her absence, Mercy would clean the school.

I had looked forward to meeting Mercy when I first moved to Blubber Bay. I imagined that as the only two teachers in the area we would have a lot in common, that we could share ideas and stories about life in a one-room school. Also, I was anxious to work closely with Mercy to see if we couldn't help her son learn to read.

Wilson needed to be assessed by an expert in learning disorders just as desperately as Timothy Davidson needed skin grafts on his legs, but like Timmy's mother, Mercy was opposed to taking her son "out." It wasn't because of the expense, which they could absorb. Rather, it was a fear and a distrust of the big, outside world, and what it might tell her that she didn't want to hear.

Mercy had come to teach in the Blubber Bay School as a young girl of nineteen. She'd worked for one year as a teacher, and then married Bob Goodman, George and Sylvia's only son. Bob was a quiet, colorless man. A fisherman and a logger like his father, Bob was honest and hard-working, but he lacked the vivacity and gregariousness of his parents. At our monthly prayer meetings he seldom said a word, although he'd bring in an arm of firewood when needed or help to tie up a visiting boat.

Mercy was a relaxed and good-natured woman. At one time she might even have been pretty. But years of her own good cooking and lack of exercise had given her the shape of a pear, and her dun-coloured hair never looked combed. She tended to wear tight t-shirts and stretch pants that only emphasized her unfortunate contours. It was hard to think of her as the lovely Sylvia's daughter-in-law.

Mercy's style of dress and her wobbling flesh didn't bother me. If I could cook like she did, I might well look the same. It was her unwashed smell that troubled me. What made Mercy stand out as an individual in an age of good plumbing and public hygiene was her complete obliviousness to the concept of bathing.

She had her artistic side. When she wasn't baking the world's best cinnamon buns, Mercy liked to paint. She would prepare for a landscape by having photographs developed as slides. She would then beam the pictures onto her canvas, and draw around the images, applying color in the style of a paint-by-number set. These paintings were highly prized among many of the local families who considered Mercy to be almost a home-grown Rembrandt.

Between her painting hobby, her young family, and the pleasure she took in baking, Mercy really had neither the time nor the desire to return to teaching. She said as much when I asked her in so many words. But I wondered if there were others like Mrs. Campbell who believed that if only they could persuade Mercy to return to her rightful place in the classroom, education would blossom in Blubber Bay as never before.

Somehow Mercy had lost her ability to function in a civilization of paved roads, hospitals, libraries, and concert halls. It was hard to picture her as a university-trained professional. Or maybe the reason she took to Blubber Bay so readily was because she never had fit into that world in the first place. In any case, Mercy was neither a soul-mate nor a rival. She was more than content to enjoy her reputation as the Grandma Moses of Blubber Bay.

Chapter Seven

Holidays

At last it was the Christmas break. We had put on a holiday pageant at school, well attended by the community, and it was time to head out.

Donna and I took the float plane to Kelsey Bay, where Richard met us and we drove down to Victoria. We spent a pleasant week visiting friends and family, then Donna and I flew back to Blubber Bay. We were sorry to leave Richard again, but we'd be seeing him again soon. With his job contract finished, he would be sailing our trimaran up to Blubber Bay and meet us there in a few days' time.

We were lucky with our flights. On both occasions, our plane had flown on time and gotten us safely where we wanted to go. Not everyone, we were to learn, was as fortunate.

A number of men from the logging camp near Blubber Bay had flown out to Port Hardy to do their Christmas shopping a couple of days before Christmas. A storm had blown up, making it impossible for planes to fly. These men had spent Christmas day in a hotel room, and their families had to wait several days to receive fathers, husbands, and holiday gifts home again.

Even they were luckier than some others. Only a week before two planes had gone down in this area, and while the passengers on one flight had survived, everyone aboard the other plane had been killed. Hypothermia studies had shown that a half-hour was about all most people could survive in these frigid waters, even when wearing a flotation device.

There was a lot of pressure on pilots to fly when conditions were not safe, especially as bad weather often lasted for days on end. In the winter it wasn't uncommon for a week or two to go by between mail runs. A person trapped away from home by inclement weather was often doomed to spend idle days in an expensive rented room, with nothing to do but hang around the airline office and pester the pilots.

Patsy Edenshaw had a teenaged sister who was away at boarding school in Port McNeill. One Friday afternoon she was waiting to fly home for the weekend, her pet cat in a carrier box, when the wind started to blow up. The pilot decided to make a run for it, but a gust caught the small float plane as it attempted to take off, and flipped it upside down. Patsy's sister managed to free her cat from its confinement as the pilot and the Blubber Bay high school students struggled out of the plane. The humans all managed to swim back to shore, but the last the girl saw of her panic-stricken cat, it was swimming into the sunset and meowing piteously.

I understood the frustration of people who would risk their lives to get home, but I often wondered about their common sense, especially when I read the sign mounted in one of the planes I was riding in: *Do not open window over 120 mph!*

However, Donna and I did make it home safely, and we were very glad to see the familiar school building huddled in the omnipresent winter drizzle. By now we could operate the generator ourselves, as the push button had been installed, and I only had to remember to check the oil each day. Soon the teacherage was warm and cheerful again.

Sammy came by and invited us for supper. His blue tuque was pulled low over his face, and a shapeless wool jacket was buttoned over layers of sweaters, overalls, and long-johns.

"What time?" I asked.

"Don't matter. Whenever you feel like it."

The afternoon went by quickly. Once I thought I heard a

gun-shot, but I thought nothing of it. I was immersed in school books, trying to get ahead on my planning for the new year. Donna had run over to see Summer Sunshine and share Christmas news. When she returned I was startled to see that it was already growing dark outside. We took our flashlights and headed over the now-familiar trail to Potters'.

Emmy and Andy were living in their own house by now, though it still looked rough and unfinished. Emmy was expecting, so they were more concerned with fixing up a room for the baby than in finishing the outside of the house.

We knocked on Sammy's door as a dog started barking hysterically. "Come in!" yelled Ma's voice. "Sparky! Shut up that noise!"

An unfamiliar, grizzled head poked around the door. An ancient woman, stringy and bowed, stared at us. "Teacher's here!"

"Well, let her come in, Granny. God!" Ma shouted back.

Donna and I entered the warm, spacious room. It smelled deliciously of wood smoke and dinner. The round table of polished cedar slabs was set for six people.

"Hang up yer coats," said Granny. "God, Mabel, it sure is hot in here. Can't you turn that stove down?"

"If yer too hot, you turn it down. Here, make yerselves at home. Take a seat. Supper'll be ready shortly."

I sat at the table while Ma resumed her work in the kitchen. She looked frail, but that little woman was strong. Ma had told me that when she planned supper each day, she usually decided on fresh fish. She would hop into her own little skiff and go out to catch the specific kind of fish she wanted for supper that night— cod, bass, salmon, halibut. She almost always could get exactly what she wanted, knowing so well the bait that each species preferred, and where they lived.

"You sure have a lot of masks," said Donna as Sammy came into the room. "They have masks like this at the museum in Victoria."

"Yeah, well the Indians brung 'em to me. They know I'll buy 'em, so any time they need money fer liquor it's *Sam, you wanna mask*? I don't like to see 'em drinking, but what're yah supposed to do?"

"Sam's real set against drinking," Ma explained. "Won't never touch a drop."

"Yeah, well, I seen too much what it kin do. My pa, he drowned when I was jist a boy, about your age. He'd bin drinking. It gets a lot of 'em."

"That must have been hard for you," said Donna with awe in her voice.

Paddy came in. She wasn't so shy around us now, and had positively warmed up to Donna. She picked up an animal husbandry magazine, remarking, "They say you can make money off of chinchilla furs. I'm gonna try that."

"You would kill your chinchillas?" Donna asked with horror.

"Sure, that's what they're for. I've been butchering my rabbits. You want to buy any?" This question was to me.

"Okay, I'll take two. Can you cut them up for me?"

Donna shuddered, but it wasn't the first time we had bought rabbit meat from Paddy. Cooked up with *Shake 'n' Bake*, it tasted just like chicken, and was a change from the monotonous canned fare we usually ate.

"I got to castrate that ram tomorrow," Paddy announced as Ma served the supper. "He's getting real cantankerous."

"You need any help?" Sammy asked.

"Naw, I can do it."

"I heard a gun shot this afternoon," I said. "Was that you?"

"Yeah, I was trying to scare away a bear. It was after my chickens."

"Did it get any?" Donna asked.

"Yep, it did. It was a smart bear all right. Never seen anything like it. It ripped a big slash in the chicken wire with his claws, then walked around to the far end of the chicken run, as calm as you please. Then he threw himself against that side of the pen, roaring and looking like fury. Those damn chickens, they panicked and ran the other way, right through that hole in the fence. The bear just came around and picked them off as they came through. Got three of them."

"Did you kill him?" Donna demanded, eyes wide.

"Naw, he ran away too fast." We ate in silence for a few moments.

"Have some pickled beets," said Ma. "Full of vitamin C."

"No thanks," I started to say, but just then Granny interrupted.

"Vitamin C saved my life. I used to have crippling back pains five, six years ago until I read that bones are made up of vitamin C, and calcium and magnesium. I started taking four big pills of vitamin C a day and within two months my back cleared up and hasn't bothered me since. Our bodies can't manufacture vitamin C, you know. Dogs, cats, they can. But humans, and apes and guinea pigs—they're the only animals that can't. Hundreds or thousands of years ago we lost the ability by a process called mutination."

The rest of us pondered this information in silence. Ma cleared her throat. "I should take some of this pudding over to Emmy. She always likes a pudding."

"How's she feeling?" I asked, referring to her pregnancy.

"We always have girls in our family," Granny answered for Ma. "Haven't had a boy for years. I can't understand it. We just never have boys. Our sperms are stronger than the men's sperms and just overpower them. A doctor told me so."

Sammy rolled his eyes. "Did you butcher that goat?" he asked Paddy.

"What goat?" Donna asked anxiously. "Did you kill a goat?"

"Not me," said Paddy. "It was a raven. They land on their backs and peck their eyes out. It's a shame, I liked that goat."

Donna looked so sad that Sammy grabbed Morris the cat and started waving him around.

"Help! Help! Don't let the ravens get me!"

Soon Donna was giggling, and Ma invited her to dig into the candy jars. We headed home shortly afterwards, struggling through rain that thundered down in near solid sheets. It was a relief to have warm baths and slip between clean, dry sheets for the night.

#

A week later, Richard arrived. He motored into Blubber Bay late one windy afternoon, tired and soaking wet but safe. We secured the *Anna Magdalena* to our jetty and prepared to live as a family again.

Although we had lived on the boat in Victoria, we planned to stay in the teacherage for the time being. Small as it was, it was more spacious than a boat, besides being handier to the school. Nobody wanted to walk through the frigid, rain drenched fields any more often than necessary.

Chapter Eight

A Leaky Roof

On the Northwest coast it rains. Five hundred centimeters in a year is not unusual. Noah may have thought that he'd seen the ultimate in wet, but his flood was as nothing compared to the constant deluge endured by inhabitants of the temperate rain forest.

The rain leeches tannin from the soil, and joy from men's hearts. It turns the world grey and bleak for weeks on end. Solid land turns to swamp, and people live in oilskins and sou'westers.

The school room was in good shape, but the teacherage dripped. The walls bled with brown, and a leak in the livingroom plopped maddeningly into a metal saucepan. Not only that, but as January went by, the ceiling began to bulge alarmingly.

"God oh god oh god," said Sammy when he looked at it. "I think you got a problem there. You better get a maintenance crew over from that School Board of yours to look at that."

I phoned Frank, but he wasn't encouraging.

"The maintenance department is backed up for weeks," he said. "I'll put in a work order, but who knows how long it will take."

There were plenty of local men who would have been glad to do any work needed if they were paid for it, but the School Board didn't contract out their jobs that way. Since Sammy would help out for free from the goodness of his heart, it was easy to take advantage of him. I didn't want to do that.

The bulge grew. I was really frightened by now, and wouldn't let Donna walk anywhere beneath it.

And it rained.

Finally it happened. We were over in the school room one day, Richard working now as my teacher's aide, when we heard a horrible *Crack!* Rushing from the classroom, followed by our eager students, Richard was the first to see it.

The ceiling in the livingroom had collapsed under an accumulation of rain water. It had leaked through the weathered shingles and soaked the insulation, collecting in a growing puddle on the sheet of plastic that lined the thin plaster of the ceiling. The water lay on the grey tiles an inch deep, soaking into couch, books, papers, and the throw rug that Richard had brought with him. Soggy slabs of plaster lay among the debris. We stared in silence. Even our students were too awed to comment.

I phoned Frank. The radio phone was working, miraculously. When the weather was bad, that was not something we could count on.

"The roof just collapsed!" I announced tersely when we connected.

"What? Was anyone hurt?"

"We were all over in the school room," I explained more accurately. "That bulge I told you about, it gave way. The teacherage is flooded. The ceiling fell down in the living room."

"Oh no." There was a pause. "Can you still live there?"

"I don't think so. We'll have to move onto our boat." *And a good thing we've got somewhere to move to*, I thought. "A lot of our stuff is ruined."

"You'll have to itemize it and send in an insurance claim to the School Board," said Frank. "Look, I'll get on this right away. You'll hear back from me later today."

Richard kept the kids busy with music and art activities while I went over to our devastated home and tried to figure out how to clean up. The bedrooms appeared to be untouched; that was something to be grateful for at least.

A steady rain of droplets fell from the torn insulation as I tried first mopping, then shoveling the mess of wet plaster into buckets. I picked apart wet papers and laid them on the kitchen counter to dry. Magazines went into the garbage. The worst hit books didn't look as if they could be saved, but I painstakingly put paper towels between the pages, hoping they would dry without sticking together.

The grey couch had acted like a giant sponge. I didn't even try to deal with that. It was the School Board's furniture; let them worry about it!

An hour or two later, Richard came over. "Frank is on the phone," he said.

I hurried over. "The School Board is accepting full responsibility," my principal announced. They're sending a work crew over with a barge of roofing materials. They should be there the day after tomorrow."

"And what do we do in the meantime?" I asked bitterly.

"Hang in there." Static crackled and the transmission went dead. As often as we tried, we weren't able to raise Frank again.

Rainbow came over and offered to keep Donna at their house until our situation had normalized, for which I was very grateful. Then Sammy and Paddy lugged a huge bundle of plastic sheeting over the mud flats. Climbing precariously onto the roof, they tacked the plastic over the teacherage shingles, preventing any new rain water from adding to the disaster inside.

Two days later, a barge appeared at the mouth of the bay. Hurrying up to the school, Autumn Mist in tow, Rainbow announced its arrival. Throwing on boots and raincoats, we all hurried down to the waterfront to watch. I decided that this would be much more educational for my students than sitting in the classroom with math books!

The barge eased its way slowly into Blubber Bay and up to the shell beach. Despite its shallow draft, it couldn't get too close; it was still several meters out from the shore. But a crane on one side of the barge looked as if it could lift the roofing materials onto lànd.

Four workmen had come over with the barge, and Sammy soon appeared as well. A few students climbed a tree overhanging the water in order to see better, which was fine until Jason fell in. Rainbow took him down to her float house, hung his clothes to dry, and dressed him in some borrowed bits and pieces.

The men hitched a huge sling of canvas and chain around a pile of aluminum sheets, and the crane started to lift. It swung the bundle slowly over the side of the barge while my students cheered. And then, to everyone's horror and amazement, the crane began to tip, further and further in suspended slow motion. It was falling, and in a matter of seconds the man operating it would be crushed. Donna started wailing noisily while the rest of us stood riveted. Finally, at the last possible moment, the operator scooted out of his seat and around the back of the crane, just as it crashed over onto its side. The body of the crane still lay on the barge, its long tower and wires in the water. With a screech of metal, the aluminum panels slowly slid out of the sling and sank to the bottom of the bay.

Perhaps the workmen were inexperienced in this sort of thing. After considerable consultation, Sammy offered to tow over his A-frame and use the winch and tackle in his boat house to help pull the crane upright again. The machinery that made it possible for him to beach his fishing boat single-handed certainly had the capacity to right the crane; it was mainly a question of how to position everything.

By this time the children were growing chilly and restless, so we headed back to the classroom. We resumed our studies much refreshed. For folks whose biggest thrill of the day was sometimes emptying the mousetraps, this had been heady stuff!

The barge left without unloading the rest of the roofing materials. Sammy told us later that with the loss of the first pile of aluminum sheets, there wasn't enough left to do the job. Also, the men feared that the crane would just fall over again.

Angry and frustrated, Richard and I took turns trying to get through on the radio phone. Finally, a day later, Frank got hold of us.

"The School Board has decided to bring in a new teacherage," he announced. "They'll be barging in a trailer for you next week."

"They'd better send a decent crane with a work crew who knows what they're doing," I retorted.

"Don't worry. Just decide where you want them to put it."

Despite the dilapidated condition of our old teacherage, I was the first teacher in years who had not demanded or begged for a replacement. It was true that the place was ugly and impossibly small, and I didn't like the holes that let in large numbers of mice, spiders, and carpenter ants. Perhaps because we had the alternative of living on our trimaran, I was even reluctant to have a new trailer brought in. I didn't want the School Board to put our rent up, but even more important, I couldn't imagine what part of our small school yard we should sacrifice.

As it happened, we weren't given a lot of choice in the matter. The School Board hired Sammy to use his bulldozer to build up the shell beach into a ramp that would extend out into the bay, so that the trailer could be pulled off the barge that brought it without having to be lifted over the water.

Early the next morning, just after dawn, we were awakened by Sammy's bulldozer driving across the mud flats, taking advantage of the low tide. He drove up the bank behind the generator shed, roaring ponderously down the playground, leaving great caterpillar tread marks behind him. He then set to work building up the shallow, gently-sloping white beach into a raised, level platform.

A few days later, at high tide, an immense barge eased its way into Blubber Bay and up to the beach. It had to do some tricky maneuvering in the limited space. The barge not only held a three-bedroom trailer and the huge crane that would ease it onto land, but it had a lot of space left over besides.

The workmen looked over our schoolyard and proposed setting the trailer right in front of the school building, where they could hook it into the school's sewage and electrical systems. I objected vehemently, pointing out that this would effectively block all view of the schoolyard. Finally the workmen were persuaded to deposit the trailer at the far end of the playground, where it would take up most of our small and lumpy baseball diamond.

The job of lifting a trailer weighing several tons onto land was a tricky business, especially as trailers are rather flimsy boxes. If roped around the middle, for instance, they will simply buckle and break under the strain. Using a series of levers, the men carefully lifted the trailer one end at a time, supporting it all the while with heavy beams. It was fascinating to watch them, dwarfed by the barge and huge machinery, moving this great unwieldy object around.

The weather was good, and it was fairly warm for late January. We were thoroughly enjoying the novelty. My students were making an uncommon amount of noise, but so long as they stayed out of the way of the trailer and the workmen, that was fine with me. I hadn't noticed a motor boat drive up, or the approach of a woman with two boys in tow.

"You the teacher?"

I jerked around, startled. "Yes, that's me."

"These are my boys, Bradley and Derrick. We just moved here. I expect my children to go to school to learn. I've told them they must listen to you and do what you say. They know they don't have to like their teacher, but they do have to learn." My jaw must have dropped; the woman took advantage of my silence to turn on her heel and march off.

"Well, hello boys," I finally managed to say. "Did you bring any books or supplies with you?" I could see that they had nothing in their hands, and no packs on their backs.

"Well, we can worry about that later. What grades are you in?"

The boys shrugged without answering.

"Bradley and Derrick, isn't it? Can you tell me what your last name is?"

Again the boys shrugged, shaking their heads.

"How old are you?"

They didn't appear to know. I had no names, no information

about their past schooling. I didn't know where they lived. I wasn't even sure if legally I could be held responsible for them. But here they were. I would have to phone Frank.

The boys turned up each morning, and I let them stay. What was the alternative? As Frank pointed out, I could hardly leave them to stand outside all day in the winter rain. I tried to catch their mother when she drove in each day, but she was so quick with her boat, and so oblivious to my gestures, that she always got away before I could talk to her.

Eventually, based on size, I placed Bradley in grade seven and his brother in grade four. Since they didn't seem to learn much, perhaps grade placement didn't matter. The months went by, and after a while we forgot the oddness of their arrival.

And then one day, the boys didn't come to school. We didn't think anything of it; absenteeism was high among some families. But later that afternoon, a police boat drove up. Two uniformed constables appeared at the classroom door. It turned out that they had been hunting the Hicks family for months, and that the parents had a long criminal record. We never learned what they had done, or heard what became of them. I've often wondered about poor Bradley and Derrick. They were contentious and uncommunicative during their months with us, but I hated to see them go.

Chapter Nine

Spring

Bird song and flowers in bud? No such harbingers of spring stir the rain-sodden souls of the hardy Blubber Bay stock. No, for us it is toads and nettles that soothe the cabin-fevered brow and relieve the tensions brought about by light deprivation and the pervading damp.

The arrival of our trailer didn't exactly spell the end of winter, but it was the start of better days for Richard, Donna and me. We moved into our new home as soon as some structural damage had been repaired. Despite all their care, a trailer isn't much more than a glorified shoe box, and a couple pieces of siding had torn loose. The workmen were able to tear off the damaged portions with their bare hands. Inside we could see the supporting trusses; one by two inch pieces of pine held together by staples.

However, we felt much more at home in the trailer than we ever had in the old teacherage. The floors were carpeted, and there were curtains at all the windows. True, there were holes in the linoleum and cracks around the window frames leaked sporadically. But it was considerably more presentable than the teacherage had been. Also, it was bigger. Richard had an office for his writing, and the spacious kitchen and livingroom were much more tastefully finished.

We still couldn't use the toilet or other plumbing in the trailer. Sammy said that we'd need a septic tank. Three weeks later the

School Board barged one over, and Sammy spent a weekend driving around the school yard in his bulldozer, tearing up the oozing mud until he had the tank and pipes installed. He filled in the holes as best he could, but it was a long time before the grass grew back.

It soon became clear that the school generator was not up to powering both the school and the trailer. Our electric water heater, washing machine and drier were replaced with propane machines, and we were warned that during school hours we must not use any more power in the trailer than we could help. Electric kettles and toasters were out of the question. The old teacherage, now used for storage, was largely dismantled. Sammy made the dangerous furnace inoperable and left his sheet of plastic in place on the roof.

All of our appliances now ran on propane, which is expensive on the north coast, and there were times when we could not get it at all. When we were running low, with no prospect in sight of getting more, we had to do without hot water and clean laundry, and try to eke out the bit that was left cooking only the most necessary bits of food on the stove. Once when we ran out altogether I had to go to Ma Potter's and ask to hard boil some eggs on her stove.

Since we tried not to be wasteful, it shocked me how often we had to recycle our hundred-pound tanks. Sammy eventually discovered that we had two propane leaks under the trailer, and were losing close to half of each tank that way.

Not surprisingly, we got a phone call from a School Board member not long after we moved into the trailer. He asked how we would feel about a raise in our rent, now that our housing had been improved so dramatically. I said that I would not like it, and that we had a contract specifying that the rent should not change. This is when we were told that all our appliances would be changed to propane and that we would be paying for the propane.

I felt sorry for the School Board, though not sorry enough to pay them more rent. Stringent budget cutbacks were already under way, and moving in the trailer must have been terrifically expensive, especially given the accident to the first barge. Running a one-room school is disproportionally costly, as materials and people must be flown in at great expense.

Also, in a city there are established structures for providing services such as electricity and plumbing. In remote areas it is still very much man against nature, and nature often wins. People must use their wits to solve problems that would be straight-forward anywhere else, and a lot of time, energy, and money can be wasted that way. People try methods that fail, and they are constantly repairing systems that are too exposed to the raw elements.

Before the workmen had left on their gargantuan barge, a covered porch was built on to the trailer, and white skirting was tacked on around the outside. The trailer had to be leveled where it had sunk into the mud, but even then it couldn't have been perfectly level as anything baked in the stove turned out at an angle. The skirting was ridiculously flimsy plastic, which broke as easily as paper under any blow. Sitting as it did in a small playground with ball games constantly under way, it was soon in tatters.

#

Not long after this, we had our first visit from Hans Baker's mother. I had met Giselle in passing at the post office, but I hadn't had a chance to get to know her. Now she was upset. She wanted to know why we had put the trailer in the ball diamond.

"Hans needs his sports," she said emphatically. "He's a growing boy. He always played soccer and baseball at his last school. Your sports program here doesn't do much to challenge the boys."

"I don't actually have a sports program," I admitted. "Our children vary too widely in age. But we do have gym class. We play a lot of cooperative games."

"Boys Hans's age need competition. He'll be terribly unhappy if he can't play ball."

"He can still play ball," I reasoned, "we'll just have to move it to a different part of the playground."

"Where?" Giselle demanded with some justification. The chain link fence had been torn down during the positioning of the trailer, and Sammy's bulldozer had left the field a torn and muddy wreck. For months afterward the students tracked copious amounts of mud into the school room, although Sylvia never complained.

I finally gave up trying to mollify her and Giselle left. She still looked pretty angry.

But through all these trials, spring came. Not the spring of song and poetry. No flower buds for us! But the rain let up a little, the sun shone warmer, and best of all, the stinging nettles grew.

We didn't look for robins in Blubber Bay. Instead there were toads. They disappeared during the winter, but as soon as the weather turned warm again, there they were in all their warty glory. The tiny ones were rather appealing, but the large, fat granddaddies were nothing but gross. They were impossible to avoid when out walking at night, but the real terror was of stepping on them with bare feet. Sammy Potter had done that once, and he still shuddered when he talked about it.

I never went out without a flashlight after dark during toad season, but with or without, the rustling plops of toads flinging themselves to the right and left out of one's path would enliven the journey. They lived under the foundations of the buildings, in clumps of nettles, under the steps, and practically anywhere they could find shelter from the sun and predators. Sammy once turned over an old tub leaning against a shed and exposed close to twenty of them.

Nettles were a pleasanter gift of spring than the toads. They could sting like the dickens, but were good to eat. After a winter with very little fresh produce, nothing tasted better than a dish of steamed nettle greens, slathered with butter and salt. They were generally good to pick for four to six weeks before aphids and spit-bugs made them unpalatable, and people from miles around would come with gloves and bags to our patch of cleared ground to pick the tender tips. There was plenty for everyone, and it was a time of feasting in many households.

A high point of our school year was the annual Nettle Feast. Our students would forage through the perimeter of the school yard and meadow, searching for the sweetest young leaves, and shrieking as they stung themselves. Not everyone wore gloves. Once their plastic bags were full, they'd run with them to the teacherage, where we kept pots of water boiling on the stove, ready to steam the nettles as fast as the kids could bring them in. A light steaming was enough to remove the poison, and they tasted quite a lot like spinach.

Nobody's really lived until they've seen twenty ravenous youngsters wolfing down big plates of steaming stinging nettles, and enjoying every bite!

Chapter Ten

Neighbors

I had often wondered about the silent man whom I had seen on the deck of Rainbow's float house the first day I arrived in Blubber Bay. I suspected he must be Rainbow's husband Geoff, but I couldn't reconcile his taciturnity with her open-hearted generosity.

It was a long time before I met Geoff. He never seemed to be around during my frequent visits. On one occasion when Rainbow put on the kettle for tea, the propane stove would not work, and Rainbow sent Summer Sunshine down to ask her father to take a look at it.

The child came running back a minute later. "He says he's busy."

Rainbow just gave a little sigh and we had water instead.

Geoff was quite a bit older than Rainbow, whom he had married when she was just twenty years old and working as a waitress in town. He had divorced his first wife, who lived with their two teenaged sons in Port McNeill.

An intelligent and creative man, Geoff always had several projects underway. Unfortunately, none of them made money, and Rainbow was often hard pressed to feed her children. She foraged from the land and she had her garden, but they could not provide all the things they needed. Flour, clothing, propane and so many other things had to be paid for with money. Rainbow made the best popcorn I ever tasted, but it took me quite a while to figure out that she made it because it was cheap and filling, not just because it was tasty.

Geoff always had notions about how his projects could be turned into money-making schemes, and his ideas were good, taken for themselves. While we lived in Blubber Bay he built his own ultra-light plane. He said he could get good money from the tourists by taking them up for flights. But once the plane was built, he lost interest and I don't think he ever took up a paying customer.

Geoff had a dark room and good camera equipment, but he only once did any professional photography that I knew of. During our second year in Blubber Bay he offered to take pictures of our students and sell prints. He doubtless made a little money on that, but whether it covered his costs, I don't know.

In desperation, Rainbow turned to her own money-making enterprise, converting her little workroom into *The Blubber Bay Gallery*. The room had been her craft and hobby corner, where she made clothing for herself and the girls, and jewelry, and little knick-knacks of driftwood and shell. With her natural sense of grace and artistry, Rainbow was soon turning out very cunning and beautiful works of folk art. I bought several pairs of beautiful earrings from her.

Ma and Sammy Potter had advanced Rainbow money to buy jewelry wire, beads, tools, glue, and the other things she would need to set up shop, and one day while the children were in school Sammy took Rainbow over to town in his fishing boat so that she could purchase the items on her list. She made a sign, burned artistically into an attractive piece of cedar, and hung it where the tourists could see.

Soon she was getting enough business, in the summertime at least, to keep the family solvent. She paid back Sammy and Ma Potter, but they remained her business partners, taking her to Port McNeill not only to buy more materials, but eventually also to sell her jewelry to craft and tourist shops in town.

Each little package or box that contained one of Rainbow's

creations also carried a tiny card with information about the materials used. My favorite came with a pair of feathery white earrings that I wear to this day. They were made of "fish ivory," a small bone which certain kinds of fish have in their heads, apparently to help them balance. Many local fishermen, hearing of Rainbow's enterprise, started carefully cutting out and saving the tiny bones for her instead of just throwing the heads to the seagulls as they had always done before.

#

We had been living in the trailer for a couple of months when I met Samantha, another of our floathouse neighbors. She was wearing a patchwork jacket, denim skirt, and a handmade cap with beaded loops sewn jauntily on one side. She walked with a lanky grace, as pretty as a rose. I stepped outside to meet her and called out my usual Hello.

"I'm Samantha," the young woman replied distantly, her eyes focused over my shoulder. "I'll need the generator on this afternoon."

"You will?" I asked incredulously. "Who are you?"

"Samantha," she explained again. "I live in the float house past Rainbow's."

"Oh, I've been looking forward to meeting you!"

Samantha indicated the unwieldy plastic carrying case in her hand. "My sewing machine works on electricity. When I want to sew I use the school building."

"Well, I'm afraid today isn't going to be convenient," I apologized. "You see, we're about to leave for the weekend. My husband is already warming up the boat engine, and I was just about to lock up."

"That doesn't matter," Samantha replied loftily. "I can lock the school when I leave."

"I don't think so." I studied her for a few moments while Samantha waited, her mind on higher things. I didn't like her, but I didn't want to start trouble with a close neighbor either.

"How long do you think you'll be?"

"It's impossible to say. I'm much too spontaneous to get locked into a schedule."

Well Miss Spontaneous, I thought, *Let's see if we can compromise.*

"I'm not going to leave the classroom unlocked. The School Board expects me to be responsible for the school. But we're not using the old teacherage any more. You can work in there."

Samantha nodded stiffly, and lugged her sewing machine across the playground and up the shabby old steps. The rickety formica table was still in there, and would make a perfectly adequate sewing surface.

Richard and Donna were waiting for me, down on the *Anna Magdalena*. I decided not to start up the generator. Samantha could deal with it. For all I knew, she might be too spontaneous to get to work right away, or she might lose interest altogether. I didn't want to risk leaving the generator to run all weekend while we were away.

Locking the trailer with more than usual care, I hurried down to the jetty with a last minute bundle of raincoats and the bag with our lunch. Passing Rainbow's garden, I was reminded that Samantha had started a small garden too. Completely overgrown, the traces of it could be seen in the meadow, not far from Rainbow's neat patch. Samantha had had to abandon her agricultural enterprise when a wandering tourist had noticed that most of her plants were marijuana, and Martinette had called the RCMP to investigate. I suspected that Samantha still grew enough to keep her spontaneity in good working order, up in the hills above Blubber Bay.

#

When Richard joined Donna and me in our new home it was a relief from several points of view. The four months of living apart had been hard on all of us, particularly Donna. Of the girls in the school, only Summer Sunshine and Patsy Edenshaw shared any interests with Donna, and they were both younger than she was. Given her lack of a social life, and the fact that I was her teacher as well, Donna needed a break from the constant companionship of her mother.

I was glad that Richard could take over the job as my aide in the school, given the tensions that Ricky's attitude had fostered between Charlotte and me. I thought that this would eliminate a source of conflict, but I was wrong. It just meant that the conflict moved to where I couldn't see it.

This came clear to us one day in the early spring when Richard rowed over to the resort for our mail. Richard had surprised me by becoming good friends with John and Martinette Wilson. He found them to be well educated and level-headed, and he enjoyed reminiscing with Martinette about the pleasures of the big city which they'd both abandoned in order to follow spouses up north.

On this occasion Richard came back from his mail run with lots of news.

"Martinette has got a petition going to force Sammy to remove his boat shed."

"What?" I exclaimed. "Did you sign it?"

"Of course not. She understands that we won't. It's mainly tourists and loggers who are signing it, nobody from right around here."

"There's nothing much she can do unless he decides to move it himself."

"That's true, but I imagine it's only a matter of time. And that's not all. Giselle Baker was over at the store."

"Oh?"

"I tried making conversation but she wouldn't talk to me."

"Well that's nothing new."

"No, I mean she *really* wouldn't talk to me. Not even 'Hello'."

"She must really be angry about that baseball diamond."

"I guess. I even tried complimenting her on the dress she was wearing, but she just stared at me and walked past."

"That's really rude," I said. "That woman has got problems. I wonder how Rod puts up with her."

"I don't know. Rod's a pretty nice guy."

Richard's tone of voice changed. "There's one more thing. Martinette said she wanted to warn us. Charlotte might be stirring up trouble."

"What do you mean? Charlotte and I are friends!"

"Apparently Ricky's been complaining that you mistreat him in school. Charlotte's pretty angry about it."

"I don't mistreat him! I expect him to do a bit of work now and then. She knows what I'm like in the classroom."

"Whatever. I'm just passing on what Martinette said. Do what you want with it."

#

Regardless of the warning, I found it hard to suspect Charlotte of malicious scheming. Her manner remained open and friendly, and the very weekend after this conversation she made good on an offer we'd discussed months earlier.

I'd met most of the parents of my students, but it was obvious that Mrs. Davidson would never visit the school. Charlotte had said that she'd be happy to take me to the Indian reservation in her boat, so I sent home a note with Patrick asking for permission to drop in for a few minutes. Mrs. Davidson had not written back, but Patrick and Jason assured me that it would be all right.

I was looking forward to seeing the boys in their own home, and perhaps Angelica as well, but the children were nowhere in sight when Charlotte and I turned in to a sheltered bay about a twenty minute ride from Blubber Bay. We tied up to a dock beside a couple of other motor boats, then walked up a dirt path from the beach. Four or five clapboard houses could be seen, most of them painted a weathered white.

"Patrick said their house was yellow," I said.

"There, that way." Charlotte spotted it first. We trudged along the path. I'd expected a lot of activity, a lot of curiosity, not to mention some rambunctious greetings from my students, but the place was silent.

"Where is everybody?" I asked. "They knew we were coming."

Charlotte said nothing, but knocked on the door of the yellow house. A moment later, a dark-haired woman opened the door. She looked like she was in her mid-thirties, dressed in a t-shirt and blue jeans. She didn't smile.

"Hello, I'm Susan Todd, and this is Charlotte Hill," I said. "Are you Patrick's mother?"

She nodded and stepped aside to let us enter the house. Pointing to a worn couch she said, "Sit down."

We sat in silence while Charlotte and I looked around the painfully clean and tidy living room. It was dominated by an oversize portrait on one wall of a little girl about three years old.

"What a cute little girl," Charlotte observed. "Is she yours?"

"Yes, that's Sarah. She died five years ago."

"I'm so sorry." We both murmured some sympathetic comments then sat quietly again. Mrs. Davidson didn't seem to feel much need for small talk.

"I'm enjoying teaching your boys very much," I said at last. "Where are they? I thought they'd be here."

"I sent them out fishing with their uncle."

"Oh. And Angelica?"

"She's out fishing too."

"Oh. Well they're very fine boys. Very polite, very hard working."

Mrs. Davidson nodded slightly. She still hadn't smiled or given any hint that she welcomed our visit.

"I'm a little worried about Timothy," I said. Mrs. Davidson did not give me any encouragement to continue.

"His legs seem to hurt him a lot. He's having a hard time concentrating at school."

"That's because he got burned."

"I understand he needs an operation?"

Mrs. Davidson nodded slightly, but her face was guarded.

"Is there anything we can do to help?"

"No. His uncle will take him to the hospital when he has time."

Charlotte and I looked at each other. We both knew that the conversation was at an end. We left, thanking Mrs. Davidson for letting us visit her and walked without talking back to Charlotte's boat.

"What did you make of that?" I asked at last as we motored back to the school.

"She's not much of a chatterbox, is she?" Charlotte answered. "I'd guess she doesn't want teachers or white folk meddling in her family business."

"No, you're right. I'll mention it to Frank Weston, but apart from that I guess there's not much I can do."

Why is it that the kids who need help the most so seldom get it? We tell the authorities, and sometimes help is offered, but it is never enough. And if the family is not receptive there is very little we can do. So many children slip through the cracks, though not unnoticed.

Chapter Eleven

Animals

I am fond of mice, when they are pets in a cage. But I don't like trapping them, which is an absolute necessity in Blubber Bay unless you are lucky enough to own a good cat.

Mice must be marvelously athletic, for they can get into places that defy the imagination. They climb into high cupboards with tight doors, into closed drawers, and up onto shelves that would be out of the reach of much larger animals. One mouse got into Garth Campbell's desk at school and chewed up a notebook and a glue bottle. The kids were sure that they'd find the mouse in there, stuck fast in the glue, but it had made its escape.

While we lived in the old teacherage next to the school mice were an intermittent problem, but it was when we moved into the trailer that our eyes were really opened to the possibilities of rodent infestation. Mice nested in the kitchen cupboards, using stuffing from the couch to make their beds cozy. At night time they chewed clothing that had been left on the floor.

They seemed to come in where plumbing pipes entered the building, so that's where we set most of our traps. Most mornings we had three or four little bodies to dispose of.

It is bad enough emptying a mouse trap when the wee victims are dead, but it is far worse when the mouse, as often happens, remains alive and suffering. My first experience of this came while working in the school one evening. Traps were set, and one close by my desk went off with a snap; but then, flailing and writhing, it continued to fly wildly through the air, bouncing and flipping in a most horrible manner. I fled the scene, but such episodes sometimes seemed more common than the instant death that I had naively assumed these traps dealt out.

On one occasion all of our traps had broken, worn out from overuse. In the few days before we could replace them the mice had a glorious time. I had refused to try another suggested remedy to the mouse problem, which is to set out a dish of dried potato flakes, which later swell and kill the mouse when it goes to drink. That and poison seemed too cruel, despite the ravages on our cupboards and furnishings. But when we did set out four shiny new traps less than a week later, all were filled within a half hour, and continued to attract new victims as fast as we could empty them.

I have found mouse droppings inside closed boxes and on top of free-standing filing cabinets. I discovered a nest inside a bag of Quaker oats. And I've seen a mouse walk straight up a paneled wall. Mice can do a lot of damage, and they are rather dirty and smelly, but they really are cute for all that. I would tolerate any number of mice rather than deal with one rat.

On the other hand, we saw a lot of deer too, many so eager for handouts that they would eat from your hand. They usually visited the school yard and meadow at twilight or later, but they were often seen in the daytime too. The deer of Blubber Bay tend to be small and inbred, and are inclined to be friendly even though many people do hunt them.

Despite her severe appearance, Martinette was very fond of animals. The first spring we were there someone brought her an orphaned fawn after shooting its mother out of season, and Martinette bottle fed the tiny creature and cared for it tenderly. Little Bambi was soon following her about the resort like a well trained dog, and rarely left her side.

Our favorite non-human neighbor was the school rabbit, set free by Paddy Potter to forage around the playground. When Donna and I first arrived in Blubber Bay, the resident rabbit was a fawn-colored specimen named Spud. Spud would allow himself to be petted, but tended to be nervous since he was often chased by dogs or little boys. The poor fellow met a sad end that Christmas while we were away in Victoria. Apparently he was weakened by the cold, damp weather and fell prey to a raven or an eagle. The Potters found what was left of his body and disposed of it before our return.

A few months later, once the trailer was moved in and spring had made the playground more inviting, Paddy brought over another rabbit. This one was a shade darker than Spud and a good deal tamer once he got used to his new home. This may have been because our rabbit-chasing students had grown up somewhat, but many attributed it to a superior personality. In fact Dups, as we called him, was a most unforgettable rabbit. He was an unashamed beggar, and soon became immensely fat. He would tag around at our heels, even following us up the porch steps if he felt ignored. His favorite food was apples, although he would settle for many other things.

Weekends were hard for Dups, for with school out of session his diet became depressingly dull. One weekend he absolutely craved an apple, but I had none to give him. I tried him on carrot tops, and then on half a potato, but he only sniffed at them disdainfully. He obviously thought we were awfully stupid or hardhearted, because his begging would have eclipsed the skill of a professional mime in getting the message across. Finally, after two days of this, I managed to get an apple for him. I called his name and waved it alluringly, and Dups came galloping over. He wriggled with ecstatic delight when I gave it to him, and ate the whole thing at one sitting.

There were a few things that Dups enjoyed at least as well as apples, but he didn't often get them as they were not considered rabbit food by any except himself. I accidentally dropped a blueberry square from my lunch on the ground one day and left it there for the crows, but Dups found it first. He sniffed it with astonishment and joy, then devoured it as fast as he was able, perhaps fearing that it would be taken away from him.

Dups was brave, although he ran when there was good reason. The Potters' dogs knew better than to chase animals, but most dogs were not so well behaved. There were enough of them around to give Dups his exercise. But when he did not consider a situation life-threatening, Dups stayed right where he was, even if a football game was milling about him. A flying tackle might narrowly miss him, but he'd go placidly on eating whatever tidbit had caught his fancy, and scarcely twitch an ear.

One spring day two or three students had left apples and carrots from their lunches out for either the rabbit or the deer, I can't remember which, but both species clearly thought it was for them. We had scarcely come inside after the one o'clock bell when a deer emerged from the trees just as Dups was making a beeline for the fodder. They reached it at about the same time, and then a comic battle was on. Dups would grab an apple and attempt to run away with it, the deer would butt him gently with its head and pick up the apple itself. Dups would wait until the deer was eating or distracted, then run in and grab the apple again. He rarely got more than a bite or two before the deer had it away from him, and deer take much bigger bites than rabbits do. Both rabbit and deer tried bounding and kicking for effect, but neither was out for blood, so they carried on until a second deer came along and finished the items under dispute.

Aside from the deer, we didn't see many wild animals. There were a few squirrels in the trees, but we seldom saw any of them. We didn't *want* to see wolves, and there wasn't much else. Eagles, ravens, and hawks, as well as the ever-present crows were often around, and sometimes there would be a bear.

Donna, Summer Sunshine, and Wilson Goodman were playing on the shore one day after school. They had rowed across the bay in our yellow dingy to the Potters' homestead, and were quite unaware of a bear just a couple of meters away from them until Paddy called out a warning. They tumbled into the dingy and were soon away, and probably the bear was as startled as they were. Although bears generally prefer to avoid people, a few were attracted every year by Paddy's livestock. Paddy shot one of them the first spring we were there, and cured its hide to hang on her wall.

For those who knew what they were doing, the north coast could feed you well. Fish of all kinds were abundant: herring, salmon, halibut, and cod. Until I met Ma Potter I had thought that fishing was a hit-and-miss sport, depending more on luck than skill. But it turned out that most of the local fishermen and women were so experienced that they could go out in the late afternoon, decide what kind of fish they wanted, and catch it. But already, in the early eighties, a lot of them were commenting that salmon and oolichan stocks were down. Sammy predicted that in another ten years the salmon would run out altogether.

Emmy and Andy had founded one of the first salmon hatcheries on the north coast, with a government grant. Their goal was to build up wild stocks and to help maintain the fish population. To do this they netted spawning salmon out of local streams, and hatched the eggs in tanks. The fry were nurtured until they had a chance of fending for themselves, then released as good-sized fingerlings into their home stream. Their success rate had been good so far, though the real test would be to see how many salmon returned to spawn in years to come.

Crabs were plentiful. They were the largest and most succulent I had ever tasted. Sylvia Goodman often brought us gifts of crab when she arrived to clean the school, and she canned dozens of jars full every year. She brought us other things to try too: ducks, herring eggs and deer meat. I cooked the deer meat in a stew and didn't tell Donna or Richard what it was, but I could scarcely eat it myself, so Sylvia didn't bring us game any more after that. The herring eggs tasted like salty rubber, but Sylvia's husband George was fond of them.

Clams were almost ridiculously easy to procure. I learned this when I dropped in on Rainbow for a cup of tea one day, to find the family getting ready to go clam digging. Donna was keen to go with them, so we piled into their small runabout and motored out to a small rocky islet just outside the mouth of Blubber Bay. At low tide a few sandy patches appear, and Geoff scraped at these with a bent pitchfork. Every forkful unearthed clams, ranging in size from small walnuts to huge dinner-plate monsters.

Ignoring the big, tough horse clams, Rainbow snatched at the tasty butter clams while Geoff scraped, and within a few minutes they had enough for several meals. The clams were washed then hung over the side of the Hurley float house in a large bucket aerated with holes for the tide to wash through. This kept the clams alive and good to eat for a couple of weeks easily, and at any time they could be steamed, chowdered, frittered, or chopped into burgers.

Growing up in Victoria, a favorite springtime wild food had been camas, but these tall blue flowers with their tasty bulbs did not live so far north. Wild onions could be had, however. During our first late spring in Blubber Bay, a large group of people went picnicking to a nearby group of small, pretty islands called the Birdwoods. Everyone had taken a hearty picnic lunch except for Patsy Edenshaw's family. They motored over with only a small bag of flour. While the rest of us unpacked thermoses, napkins, and plastic-wrapped packages, they calmly built a fire, dug a few clams and picked wild onion, made chapatis, and soon had such a tasty meal ready that they ended up sharing with everyone on the beach.

Behind the school grew a large patch of spearmint which was raided by much of the community every spring to make tea for the coming winter. We picked our share too. We found the best way for us was to cut the stalks with scissors and hang them in bundles from the ceiling of the teacherage to dry. The first year we did this, Donna and I picked and hung so much that our eyes stung from the mint fumes whenever we walked into the teacherage. Even at that we had used up all the leaves by the time mint season rolled around the following year.

Although Richard and I were not interested in living off the land, there were many people homesteading around Blubber Bay whose whole purpose in being there was to live as close to nature as possible. These folks were of two types. The first were people like the Potters, the Edenshaws, and the elder Goodmans. They knew the land thoroughly, with no romanticism. They had all the skills and knowledge needed to survive, but they valued the comforts of technology. Most were of my parents' generation. They were tough and practical, with no illusions, lots of neighborly concern, and genuine wisdom.

The second group of pioneers were largely Americans who had grown up during the sixties, and were still disillusioned with technology and "the Establishment." They tended to be somewhat romantic about their return to subsistence living, and to be guided by a mixture of mysticism, Eastern spiritualism, and religious superiority. Many had learned the skills of the true pioneers without learning their attitudes. While I liked and respected many of the people I met with this background, more often they seemed like pretty poor imitations of what they were trying to be.

One couple who almost made it work were Driftwood Dan and Glory. Driftwood Dan kept all of his possessions in a kayak. He could live through the winter in a hut built of driftwood and stray boards. So long as he had a source of fresh water, a little flour, and a sharp knife he didn't need much else. He was living like this when Glory first came to the area and met him. She was captivated by Dan's simple lifestyle, so different from what she had known in California. Glory adopted the life with enthusiasm, and all was going well until they had their first child. Glory found that she needed a roof over her head and a home base, but Dan found it hard to settle down to the more conventional lifestyle. Eventually they separated, Dan to return to his kayaking, and Glory to bring up her two children in a house, and with a pay cheque, in Alert Bay.

Chapter Twelve

A Nasty Rumor

Perhaps I should have confronted Charlotte about the rumors which Martinette claimed she was spreading, but it was hard to know what to believe. Charlotte was a warm and jolly person, always friendly, whereas I found Martinette to be cold and hatchet-faced. I knew that Sammy and Rainbow distrusted Martinette, and I didn't feel inclined to trust her either.

Richard on the other hand liked Martinette and had very uneasy feelings about Charlotte. We both liked Sammy Potter and Rainbow Hurley. I remembered Frank Weston's advice to avoid taking sides in the community, so we tried to do our jobs well and to be pleasant to everyone, regardless of our private feelings.

And life went on. Samantha, our spontaneous neighbor, moved to Port McNeill, and an artist named C.J. Brown moved into her floathouse. Rainbow soon was offering her paintings for sale alongside the jewelry and other crafts in *The Blubber Bay Gallery*.

Martinette continued to collect signatures for her petition, and Sammy stopped going to pick up his mail. His daughter Emmy would go to the resort once a week to pick up letters, but the rest of the family never set foot in Martinette's store. Every weekend Sammy would make a run to Port McNeill in his fishing boat, and take along anyone who wanted to shop "in town" with him.

Mercy Goodman filled in for Sylvia on the occasions when our school janitor had to be away. George was having some health problems, so he and Sylvia had to make regular visits to town to see a heart specialist.

Throughout the months of tight-roping through escalating community tensions, I looked forward to our monthly prayer meetings. Although Richard and I didn't pray, we felt safe in the friendly atmosphere of the Lemieux-Goodman get-togethers.

We were getting to know Reverend and Mrs. Smith better too. Like her husband, Marjorie Smith was always dressed as if for church in town. I never saw him without a suit, nor her without a dress and hat, although they lived on a small boat that needed constant maintenance. Knowing that they had worked in boat ministries for most of their lives, I once asked Mrs. Smith how she had managed to bring up a family under those conditions. She explained that "the Lord had not blessed them with children."

Sometimes Patsy Edenshaw's family joined us at these gatherings, to Donna's delight since she rarely saw Patsy outside of school hours. It was Mrs. Edenshaw who warned us in the late spring of a rumor that would be one of many to trouble our lives throughout our remaining year in Blubber Bay.

#

After each sermon, before we broke for a pot-luck lunch, Reverend Smith would ask whether any of us had special prayers. Sylvia Goodman and the Lemieux's often suggested prayers with someone specific in mind.

On this occasion, however, Mrs. Edenshaw spoke up. I was surprised because I'd never heard her ask for a prayer before. I was even more surprised when she said, "Let us pray for the Todd family."

Richard and I stole a quick glance at each other. For us? Were our sins that apparent?

But Mrs. Edenshaw continued, "It may be nothing, but Giselle

Baker visited me yesterday. There's a first time for everything I guess. She wanted me to know that Richard here made a pass at her when they met over at the resort."

"You did?" I asked.

Richard looked bewildered. "I don't think so. I couldn't have. I told you what happened."

"The problem isn't with what you did," Mrs. Edenshaw said. "It's with what Giselle is saying. In her mind you came on to her, or that's what she wants to believe."

"But it doesn't make any sense," Richard protested. "I hardly said two words to her."

"It might make more sense than you think," Pierre interrupted. "Rod's left."

"Left?"

"I saw him last week. He said good-bye. Said he was heading down-island to look for work."

"Then that could explain quite a lot."

"Let us pray," Reverend Smith said. "Dear Lord, protect with your mercy our dear brother and sister Richard and Susan from slanderous tongues. Let us keep our feet upon the path of righteousness. Help us to forgive those who would harm us. Guide us in the ways of truth. And help our neighbor Giselle in her time of trouble. Amen."

"Amen," we all repeated, and for once Richard and I were as fervent as everyone else.

#

Three floathouses faced the resort across Blubber Bay. C.J. Brown lived in the second house past the Hurley's, but the third cedar house had sat empty for years. Rainbow told me that it belonged to an old prospector who had retired in that area, but he left to live with family when he grew too old and feeble to care for himself. The house had not been lived in since.

Geoff and Sammy kept an eye on the house so that it didn't break loose from its moorings or attract squatters who might move in. Apart from that nobody thought much about the house at all, so it was a surprise when Summer Sunshine arrived at school one morning with the news that we had a new neighbor.

"Her name Is Nancy," Summer Sunshine told us. "Mom helped her move in."

I looked forward to meeting Nancy. Since Rainbow had welcomed her, she must have a right to the house she was living in. It was quite exciting. Including ourselves, this brought the population of Blubber Bay up to a whopping sixteen people.

The next weekend I decided to go and introduce myself, but I didn't have to go very far. Nancy was in the forestry park, chatting with Rainbow who was preparing her garden plot for planting. I invited them both up for tea but Rainbow shook her head with a quick smile that might almost have been of relief. She wanted to finish her work in time to get home and prepare lunch for Geoff and the girls she said.

Nancy chattered non-stop while we walked back to the trailer.

"I flew up from Kelsey Bay on Tuesday. What a ride! I couldn't bring much with me because I hitch-hiked from Parksville, but I don't need much.

"The house really belongs to Grandpa Neils. He's in a nursing home now. Oh, is this your place? The ground is so muddy!"

We picked our way across some old boards and sheets of plywood that Sammy and Richard had laid in a path up to the porch. Richard and Donna had gone hiking up the hill, so Nancy and I had the trailer to ourselves.

"Mint tea or Earl Grey?" I asked.

"Oh, mint tea please. Did you grow it yourself? I plan to grow everything for myself once I'm settled in. Do you have a garden?"

"No, Rainbow is the gardener around here. Sugar?"

"Oh no, refined sugar is so bad for you. Do you have any honey?"

I searched the cupboard for honey while Nancy chattered on.

"I deliberately moved here in the spring so that I could start a garden. I want to live like the old homesteaders did years ago. I should be able to put enough aside to keep me going through the winter, don't you think?"

"I don't know," I said. "Do you have any experience in homesteading?"

"No, but I brought an axe with me, and I know how to identify edible plants. I've made a couple of meals off of the land already!"

"Well, that's a start." I apologized as I put the teapot on the table. "I only have powdered milk, but I don't suppose you want milk in mint tea anyhow."

Nancy shuddered. "I never drink milk. Dairy products are loaded with cholesterol, you know. And don't even get me started on factory farming. I'm a vegan."

"A vegan?"

"Like a vegetarian, but I don't eat any animal products, not even cheese or eggs."

"You mean you're not going to fish or dig clams?"

"Nope."

Nancy had short, curly hair and a wizened face. But she talked and moved like someone very young, so it was hard to tell how old she really was. She wore sandals and flowered overalls. A strange odor surrounded her, and I found myself trying to identify it as we talked. It was almost like garlic emanating from her pores.

"I'd love to volunteer in the school," Nancy went on. "Kids really like me, you know. Rainbow told me you're the teacher."

"Well, we'll see. I have an aide already, but we might be able to use a volunteer every now and then." Privately, I wasn't sure how useful Nancy would be in the classroom.

As we drank our tea, Nancy told me about protest marches she had taken part in across the country. She had hitch-hiked as far away as Ottawa to join a rally on Parliament Hill.

"Big business is ruining our economy," she told me. "Multi-national corporations have the government in their pocket. And as for their treatment of the poor, don't get me started."

"Okay," I agreed. That was a suggestion I'd be happy to obey.

Chapter Thirteen

Living on a Boat

We were very happy that we had our trimaran to move onto when the ceiling in the teacherage collapsed. Without the *Anna Magdalena* to live in I'm not sure what we would have done. Perhaps neighbors would have offered to put us up, or we could have rented a room at the resort across the bay. Neither alternative would have been as comfortable as our boat.

We had bought the twelve-meter Piver trimaran three years earlier when we grew tired of paying escalating rents in Victoria. At that time we were not yet familiar with the all too true adage that a boat is "a hole in the water into which you throw money." At the time it seemed like the perfect answer to a lot of our needs. With a boat we could travel, while at the same time staying comfortably at home. We could expose Donna to new places and a different way of life. It appealed to our sense of adventure and fun.

We bought the boat on a lucky Friday the 13th when Donna was eight years old. It was a good choice for a family, being unusually spacious inside. The three hulls made it extremely stable, and virtually unsinkable. And unlike many trimarans, the outer hulls and connecting wings had living space inside them.

For a couple of years we lived at Fisherman's Wharf in Victoria, and Donna went to the local James Bay School. We were not alone in our lifestyle. Many people, families among them, lived on a variety of houseboats, converted tugboats, cabin cruisers, cramped little sailboats, and fishing vessels. And up in the parking lot, a family with five cheerful children lived in an old school bus.

Richard and I each had an office area in one of the outer hulls or "amas," and Donna had her own private cabin behind the cockpit. It was noisy in there when the engine was running, but we had outfitted the compartment with pretty and girlish accessories, and despite its small size the room was cozy and comfortable.

The main cabin held the galley and dining area. There was a sink with a foot pump for cold running water, and ample cupboard space. All the cupboards had lips and sliding doors to prevent their contents from falling out in rough seas. The table could be pivoted out of the way, freeing up the floor space in the middle of the cabin.

A compact coat closet, the toilet or "head", and the bow cabin which we used for storing anchors and life jackets completed our living space. It was a lot of room for three people living on a boat.

As soon as we had made plans to purchase the boat, we enrolled Donna in swimming lessons at the local YMCA. By the time we moved to Blubber Bay she was swimming reasonably well; at least well enough that we no longer worried about her falling overboard and drowning. On the proud day that she could swim a hundred meters without a rest, we decided that she would no longer have to wear a life jacket every waking moment. The bulky life preservers were a nuisance; doing without felt like the freedom you get when you put away heavy snow boots after a long winter.

#

Living on a boat isn't all freedom and adventure. It is also rot and dampness and strange odors from the bilge. But above all, a boat means engine troubles.

Richard, a writer and musicologist by trade, spent much of his time lying on his back in the engine compartment under our cockpit. It was bad enough trying to keep the engine going when we lived in Victoria, but in Blubber Bay parts had to be mail-ordered from Vancouver. It was an expensive and time-consuming business. However, a working engine was a vital necessity, for while we often referred to "sailing" the boat, the sad truth was that we usually motored wherever we wanted to go.

More often than not this was due to time constraints. If the wind does not blow, or it is coming from the wrong direction, it can take a very long time to sail where you want to go. We rarely had the leisure to wait for the wind. Also, the many small islands and submerged rocks that lie between northern Vancouver Island and the mainland can make sailing a painstaking and hazardous business. You have to keep your eye on the charts and be ready to tack at a moment's notice. A large sail boat needs a lot of wide open spaces to maneuver in.

Richard and I had hit a deadhead once, a log floating below the surface of the water, and it had torn the bottom out of one of our three hulls. Fortunately a trimaran cannot sink, but the repairs had been costly and time-consuming. We'd been forced to lay up for two dull and stressful weeks in an out-of-the-way harbor where we really had no interest in being.

Richard's single-handed voyage north to Blubber Bay had been a real challenge. But if he'd had to rely on sails alone, it would have been an impossibility.

#

One afternoon after school, around the middle of May, I sat at my desk marking books and enjoying the quiet. I had sent my students down to their boats a few minutes earlier, and Sylvia Goodman hadn't arrived yet. So I was startled when Summer Sunshine burst into the classroom and screamed, "Donna fell into the water and she's crying!"

I burst out of my seat like an arrow and ran out the door, with Summer Sunshine struggling to keep up and explain what had happened.

"She fell off the boat. She couldn't get out. But Garth saved her and now she's at my house."

I ran to Rainbow's float house and let myself in. Sure enough, I could hear Donna crying upstairs, and Rainbow's gentle voice soothing her. I found them in the kitchen, Donna wrapped in towels.

Rainbow explained, since Donna's sobs prevented her from speaking.

Pierre had been late on this day, which was unusual for him. We found out later that his engine wouldn't start, and he'd had to take it apart to find out what the problem was. So while they waited, all the children except Helen and Stephanie, and Veronica and Ricky, ran about in the meadow and played on the ramp.

For some reason Donna had gone down alone onto the trimaran. Perhaps she meant to get something out of her cabin, but we kept the *Anna Magdalena* locked up when we weren't there. Running around on the deck, somehow Donna had managed to fall into the deep water.

Her swimming lessons paid off. But no matter where she tried to climb up, a hand-hold eluded her. The smooth hulls of the boat towered a good meter above the water line.

Next Donna tried swimming over to the dock. The tarry black pilings and the shadows under the dock frightened her, but she tried to find somewhere she could hang on and pull herself up. There was no way out anywhere she looked, and ugly black mussels made it hard to get too close.

By now the other children had noticed and were calling out suggestions. Most of them screamed at her to swim to shore and climb up the muddy bank, but Donna refused. The mud was deep and slimy, and full of sharp tin cans, broken beer bottles, and discarded fish hooks. Finally, shivering and weak, Donna started to cry, dog paddling in little circles as she tried to keep warm.

Garth Campbell ran down to the dock as close to Donna as he could get and reached out to her. Taking command, he ordered

Wilson and his little brother Davy to grab hold of him so that he wouldn't fall in. Donna swam to him, and he grabbed her hands, but it took the combined strength of Garth, Sylvain, and Garth's older sister Lisa to pull Donna out since the dock was so high out of the water.

Meanwhile, Summer Sunshine had run home to get her parents. Garth's twin sisters were having a great time watching from the ramp, laughing, screeching, and calling out unhelpful suggestions as the other children dragged Donna over the low railing and onto the wet planks.

Garth and Sylvain shepherded Donna up the ramp and into Rainbow's waiting arms. Rainbow had barely gotten her undressed and starting to warm up when I got there. By that time Pierre had come and gone again, doubtless to hear the story many times on his way home.

We all learned something from this incident. From then on, I always walked the children down to the dock, no matter how inconvenient it might be. Donna learned not to run or horse around on boats. And Geoff Hurley built a ladder and hung it from the end of the dock, just in case such a thing should ever happen again.

#

Nancy Jacobsen, our vegan neighbor, was intrigued that we could live on our boat. She pestered Richard until he promised to take her sailing, which we finally did one weekend late in May. She was enthusiastic about everything—the foot pump that provided our running water, Donna's cabin, the flushing "head."

But what Nancy really wanted to do was help us out in the classroom. I finally agreed to let her come in two mornings a week to read with the younger children and help coach kids with their math, even though the school year was almost over.

The first morning was memorable. Nancy arrived early, before most of the kids, and spent a few minutes chatting while she looked around the classroom.

"You don't have a lot of information on display about good nutrition or animal rights," she observed. "I could send for some posters from PETA if you like,"

"Thanks. You can if you want." I tried to use an unencouraging tone of voice.

I stepped outside to watch the children play for a few minutes before I rang the morning bell, leaving Nancy alone in the classroom. I had put a proof-reading exercise on the board for the senior students to copy into their notebooks. We'd been studying how to self-edit written work and I was hoping they'd find all the corrections that needed to be made.

Richard came out of the trailer, my signal to ring the hand bell that we used at such times. As the kids came in and hung up their sweaters, Nancy met me at the door with a big grin.

"I fixed that work you put on the board," she said. "You made all kinds of mistakes. I didn't think you'd want the kids to see that!"

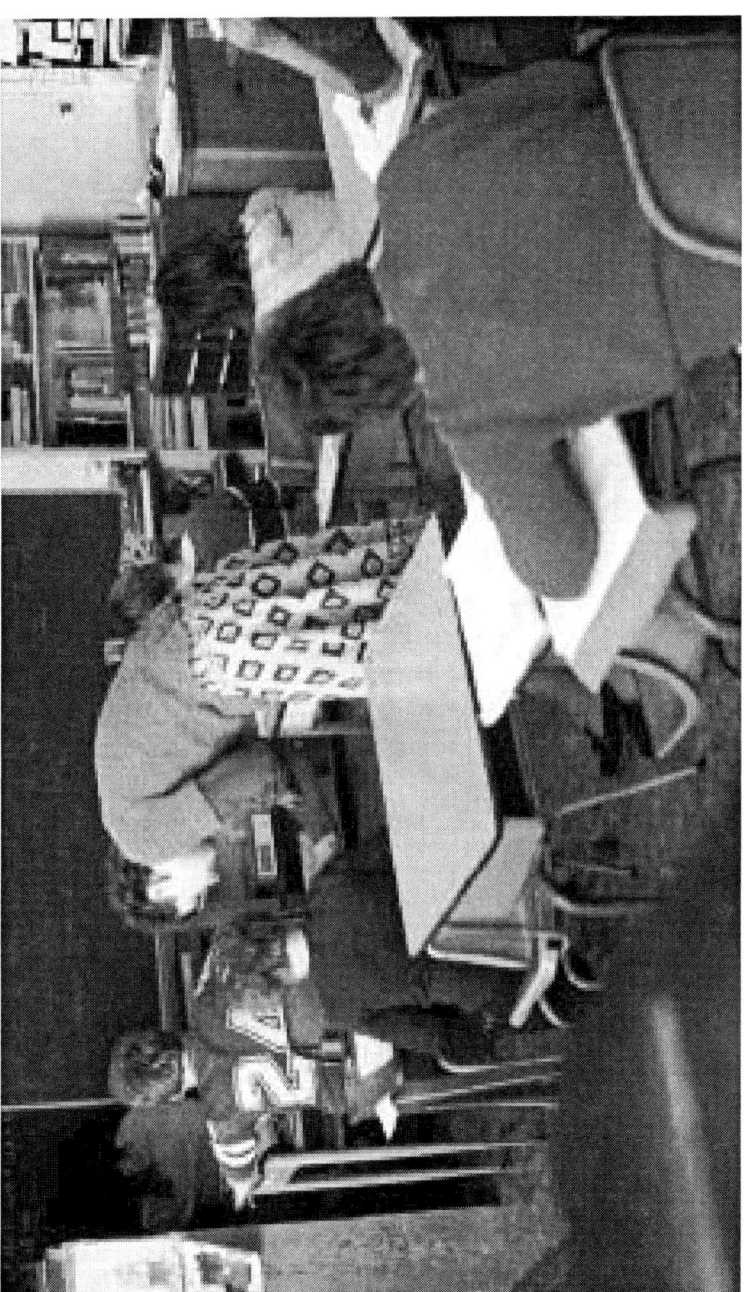

Chapter Fourteen

Students

I was doubtless foolish given the problems we were already having in the community to consider teaching a course on Sex Education, but as the months went by it began to seem like something the older girls really needed to know. Lisa Campbell was a pretty girl and well into puberty, but very ignorant and vulnerable. Given her craving for attention and affection, I figured she'd be a sitting duck in a logging camp where girls were often pregnant and sometimes even married in their mid-teens.

Stephanie Potts on the other hand was already confident of her ability to attract men. She flaunted her sensuous young body and often wore clothes that showed off just a little more skin than was appropriate for school. Stephanie had very large eyes with thick lashes, and a quantity of dark, wavy hair that she liked to wear loose. She would likely be a very beautiful young woman, physically at least.

Her older sister Helen was unfortunately just the opposite. Her hair was a nondescript color, lank and thin, and her skin was pale and blotchy looking. A sparkling personality would have compensated for her looks, but poor Helen was shy and awkward. I had tried to draw her out and build up her self-confidence, but living in the shadow of her younger sister had convinced her that she was dull and worthless. The first young man to overlook her appearance was likely to have an easy conquest.

108

Angelica was pretty and she had a cheerful, out-going personality. But I wasn't sure that life on her secluded reservation was preparing her to be a fulfilled adult woman either.

After consulting with Frank Weston, I decided to teach the course to all the children in grades 5 and up, with Richard taking the younger children for alternate activities during the same time. Children in grade 4 were given the option of taking the course if the parents particularly requested it.

To my surprise, all of the children except Sylvain Lemieux brought in notes giving them permission to take the course. Sylvain's mother Denise wrote that she'd prefer to teach him herself at home, in a Christian context. That was fine with me as I knew she'd do a good job.

Stephanie handed me her permission slip with a supercilious air. "I don't know why I have to take Sex Ed," she said as I added her paper to the others on my desk. "My mother already told me everything I need to know."

"She did?" I asked. "I'm pleased to hear that." Privately I wondered whether so many parents had agreed to the course out of relief that they might not have to address these issues with their children themselves.

#

One senior student who missed my lessons on Sexuality was Danny Storto. As Veronica Hill and Frank Weston had warned me, he attended school only often enough to keep his name on the register until he was old enough to drop out. It was hard to imagine Danny as a logger. For one thing, he sucked his thumb constantly.

Danny Storto was thirteen years old and in grade 8 when I first met him. He arrived at school a few days late and slipped into his desk so quietly that I might not have noticed him if the other students hadn't pointed out his presence.

"Danny's here! Teacher, that's Danny."

"Hello Danny," I said, but he looked away. I supposed he was shy. Certainly he was never domineering or aggressive despite being the oldest boy in the school. He seemed to wish he could become invisible.

Danny was able to read and write, and he could do the basics in math. But he was uncomfortable when Charlotte or I tried to work with him. He would turn his face away, and lean his body out of contact range. Like Helen, he spoke in monosyllables.

I never really got to know Danny. Early in my second year at Blubber Bay School he dropped out and got a job at the logging camp. He was fifteen years old. Helen dropped out the year after, and I often wondered whether they made a couple.

#

Designing my Sex Education lessons was tricky. I didn't want to expose the younger children to subject matter they weren't ready for, but I did want to prepare the older ones for the hazards that lay ahead in their teenage years. Sometimes I had to ignore the protests of my grade 4 students and send them off with Richard while I got slightly more graphic with the older ones.

The students themselves never worried about how graphic they were being, and despite my concerns about what the nine-year-olds were occasionally hearing, their questions and comments only confirmed my conviction that they needed the information I was teaching. For instance, there was the day when Angelica asked whether sex between a human and a dog could produce a baby. It seemed to be a stunt that she'd either considered, or heard of someone else trying.

While not happy with the direction the conversation was taking, I had promised that any honest question would get an honest answer. I'd also encouraged the older students to write private notes about questions that might make the younger children uncomfortable, so that I could answer them privately. But most of them seemed to feel a surprising lack of embarrassment while discussing situations that I would much rather have avoided.

Stephanie was able to answer Angelica's question. Despite her assertion on the first day that she already knew it all, Stephanie had been an attentive pupil throughout this course.

"No, different animals can't have a baby," she said firmly. "The chromosomes aren't the same so they can't match up to make a baby."

Stephanie was ready with all the answers, and usually she was right. However, one day Patrick asked why some babies were boys and some were girls.

"My mom told me that," said Stephanie. "There are two tubes that the eggs come down to the woman's uterus."

"The Fallopian tubes," I nodded.

"Eggs that come down one of the tubes turn into girls, and eggs that come down the other tube turn into boys."

"Uh, well that's not quite right," I temporized.

"My mom told me so." Stephanie looked at me challengingly.

"Well, maybe your mom got a little mixed up at that part." I explained about X and Y chromosomes, but I could see that the kids thought Stephanie's explanation was more convincing.

I tried to teach my students that it was okay to wait until they were adults before experimenting with a partner, and that they had the right to say *No*. I hoped to persuade them that drinking and smoking were harmful to a developing baby, but here again I met scepticism. Most of their mothers smoked, and many of them drank as well. As my students pointed out, none of them had suffered as a result. But I wondered, how much more might Helen Potts have been, or Lisa Campbell or the twins, if their early years had been different? And how much of a future did the bright and the beautiful have, with no education, no knowledge of the world outside, and the likelihood of becoming mothers before growing up themselves?

#

Most of our lessons were more upbeat. Toward the end of the school year we prepared a drastically abridged version of *Hamlet* and invited the community to attend. Stephanie played Ophelia with a dynamic passion that one seldom sees in that character, while Sylvain Lemieux took the title role as the young prince. Donna was Queen Gertrude, with Patrick Davidson as Claudius. Everyone had a prime part, and when Garth Campbell in his role as Laertes stabbed Hamlet in the final scene, the audience was roused to a standing ovation.

The last day of school we had a Track and Field Event, and again we invited the community. I had never encouraged competitive sports as with such a wide range of ages it would have been impractical. Instead, gym activities throughout the year stressed cooperation and teamwork. It paid off as adults and children of all ages participated in funny activities and absurd races.

On the whole, it had been a good year. Most of our students had made fine progress academically. Our worries about Charlotte or Giselle creating problems had come to nothing, or so it seemed. Any lingering misunderstandings would surely blow over during the summer. And my dangerous experiment in teaching Sexual Responsibility had not resulted in the expected cries of outrage from scandalized parents.

#

Richard beached our trimaran beside Sammy's boat shed and scraped the bottom, giving it a new coat of toxic copper paint. We checked the bilge for dampness and rot, liberally salting the narrow spaces under the floor boards. Soon we'd have to lock up the classroom and the trailer, load our possessions aboard the *Anna Magdalena*, and set sail to Victoria for the summer.

The boat was a little damp since we hadn't been living on it, so I took pains to air our bedding. Nancy came over to help. With her usual enthusiasm she carried up towels and blankets, strewing them haphazardly around the deck. While I ran to pick them up and secure them with clothes pins to the rigging, she hauled up

Donna's foam mattress. Propping it against the cabin wall, she disappeared below again.

I tried to think of a tactful way to tell Nancy that I really didn't want any more help when the wind started gusting. Little waves raced up the bay toward us, and the towels flapped. Like an ungainly bird, the mattress lifted into the air and sailed across the mud flats, landing at last in knee-deep water.

Hardly trying to hide my displeasure, I waded after it. But not even Nancy could completely destroy my good mood. For concerts and movies, friends and family, ice cream, swimming, book stores and supermarkets awaited us. A summer of civilization!

Chapter Fifteen

Cougar!

By late August we were back in Blubber Bay and ready for another year. All of our students would be returning except for Danny Storto and Angelica Davidson, who had moved to Alert Bay. On the other hand we had two children coming into kindergarten, Autumn Mist Hurley and Wilson's little brother, Bobby Goodman.

We had loaded our boat not only with enough food supplies to last us until Christmas, but with boxes of teaching materials as well. I brought books for the school library and costumes for our next dramatic production, which I hoped would be another adaptation from Shakespeare.

The first thing we noticed when we motored the *Anna Magdalena* to the school jetty was that Sammy Potter's boat shed was gone. The white shell beach looked exposed and empty. Martinette had won her battle at last.

We moved a few boxes up to the trailer and looked around. Someone, probably Sammy or Paddy, had mowed the grass in the school yard quite recently. The generator shed had a new coat of paint and the broken skirting around the trailer had been repaired.

Dups hopped up to meet us as if we'd never been away. Crows strutted around the field and a kingfisher flew to the top of a tree beside the school, holding a small fish in its beak. It was good to be back.

Donna wanted to see Summer Sunshine, so she ran off to the Hurley's floathouse, and Richard rowed over to the resort to pick up our mail. I remembered how strange it had felt to arrive on my own the year before. Blubber Bay was home now, and we were eager to find out what had gone on while we'd been away.

With this in mind I walked down the path to visit with Rainbow. The girls were running around in the park, playing with bubble wands that we'd brought from town. Negotiating the narrow ramp to Rainbow's floathouse, I looked across the bay.

Richard was on his way back, and we waved. As I watched, a sudden gust of wind whipped a letter that he'd been reading out of the dingy and across the water. Richard turned the boat in an effort to retrieve it, but the letter sank beneath the waves and we never found it again. He told me later that it had been from an old friend who'd moved to Calgary the year before. The letter was meant to re-establish contact and give us the new address, but it was lost for good. We often regretted losing that friend.

Rainbow took a while to answer the door. She explained why as we went inside.

Her neighbor, C.J. Brown, had fallen from a cliff while climbing the hill behind their houses earlier that month. She'd been looking for a good view of Blubber Bay so that she could paint it from above.

Fortunately Geoff had been working outside on his ultra-light and saw her fall. He sent Rainbow to the Potters for help, then Geoff and Sammy took C.J. to Port Hardy in Sammy's fishing boat. Her leg was badly broken, but C.J. refused to stay in the hospital in Port Hardy. It turned out that she was an American and didn't have any health insurance. So Geoff and Sammy brought her back home again once the leg was set, and Rainbow was now nursing her neighbor.

C.J. lay flat on her back in Rainbow's family room. She had been badly bruised by the fall, and her back had been injured as well. But she remained surprisingly cheerful, and was confident that she'd be back on her feet within a few weeks.

C.J.'s hospital bill was steep despite her brief stay, so the community rallied around to help. Since she was unwilling to take charity, people had started buying her art work, and Rainbow had been forced to raid C.J.'s floathouse and workshop for landscapes that hadn't yet been put up for sale in *The Blubber Bay Gallery*.

Richard and I couldn't hang a painting in our trimaran, but C.J. also decorated goose eggs provided by Paddy Potter with beautiful Ukranian designs. We bought an egg and hung it in the galley of our boat, where it swung with the bobbing of the waves for years afterward.

#

A few days later school started. Since all my students knew me already, the year got off to a very smooth start. I always found that this happened when I taught the same class for more than one year. Since they knew how I would react to misbehaviors, discipline was rarely an issue. The second year with a class was always more relaxed, with more time spent on learning.

The class had a slightly younger and more innocent ambience, too, with the addition of Autumn Mist and Bobby, and now that the Hicks boys and Danny Storto were no longer with us. The older children looked after the younger ones, reading to them and encouraging them, and modifying their outdoor play so that everyone could participate.

They were usually cooperative inside the classroom as well. We ate lunch at our desks, except on very fine days when we'd often picnic outside on the grass, sharing the best tidbits with Dups and the crows. When we ate in the classroom, everyone would wash off their desktops and do a quick clean-up before going outside for free time.

Many of the students liked to help out, and I was often hard-pressed to find enough jobs for them. Sylvia was so thorough in her janitorial duties that there was very little for us to do in the classroom. Sometimes Garth Campbell or Hans Baker would offer to empty a mousetrap, or if the generator was off kids would haul up pails of water from the beach so that we could flush the toilet. Without electrical power, there was no pump to keep the toilet tank filled.

One day a live mouse was running about in the school washroom, frightening the younger children when they went to use the toilet. Thinking that this might be a good job for one of the older students, I asked who would like to get rid of the mouse, and Stephanie Potts immediately volunteered. Eschewing all offers of help, Stephanie shooed us all outside for recess so that she could get on with the job.

It turned out that her method of choice was to take a baseball bat from the store room and bludgeon the mouse to death. The rest of us were horrified when we found out, but Stephanie was very pleased with herself. In fact, she enjoyed the task so much that I decided never to give her an animal to deal with again.

#

About a week after school had started the children were playing outside while I marked books at my desk. Normally Richard or I would be outside with the class, but on this occasion Richard had gone up the hill behind the school to check on a broken water line. I could hear the kids playing through the open windows, and every couple of minutes I'd get up to check on them.

Suddenly I heard screams, and the quiet game they were playing burst into bedlam. Flying from my chair, I reached the door at about the same time the kids started to arrive.

"Cougar! Cougar!" they screamed. Patrick and Garth were running around after the youngest children, herding them toward the school and dragging the slower ones by the hand, while the other children raced for the classroom and safety.

"Cougar? Where?" I asked.

"There! There!" They pointed toward the woods but I could see nothing.

Most of the kids were excited, a couple were frightened, and Donna was in tears. It turned out that most of them hadn't seen the cougar. The twins and Veronica claimed that they had, and Ricky Hill insisted that the cougar had been only inches from ripping out his throat, but I was a little skeptical. Maybe there had been something there. It might have been just a deer in the shadows.

But just in case it *was* a cougar, I hoped that Richard wouldn't be too long in returning. Our water pressure had fallen off to a dribble that morning, which usually meant that a coupling in the plastic pipes that led down the hill had worked themselves apart. We got our water from a stream up the hill, and the make-shift above ground tubing often leaked.

The kids were too excited to get back to work, so we sat on the carpet and shared cougar stories until lunch time. Most of the logging camp children claimed to have seen cougars lots of times, but the floathouse children and the Davidsons were more modest in their claims.

Richard finally returned and said that he'd seen no sign of a cougar. But just in case, we kept the kids inside for the rest of the day and we both walked the students to their boats after school. Donna, Bobby and Wilson stayed inside the classroom until Sylvia was ready to take the boys home.

Although Richard usually went for the mail, I decided to row over that afternoon. It was a lot of fun to row our yellow dingy across the bay on a fine day. But when I arrived at the resort, it was in turmoil. Men from the logging camp were roaring up to the dock in their motor boats, most of them with guns. Tourists watched from their yachts and from the fancy building up the hill.

Walking into the store I asked, "What's up?"

"A cougar!" Martinette said. She was much more animated than usual. Her pet fawn lay under the counter by her feet.

"Bambi and I had gone to get our lunch while John looked after the store like he always does around noon. It was quiet today, nobody coming in for gas or anything. We started walking down the hill, when I felt something behind me. I didn't think anything of it, you know. I thought it was just one of our guests walking down the hill. But then I turned, and what do you think I saw?"

"A cougar?" I guessed.

"A big one! Right behind Bambi, no further away than I am from you. I was so scared."

"What did you do?" I wasn't the only one listening to Martinette's tale. The store was full of people. Since many of them had loaded guns, that made me even more nervous than the thought of meeting the cougar on my way home.

"I grabbed up a boat hook that somebody had left there and whacked that cat right on the head."

"Lucky it didn't go for you," one of the men commented. "You should've let it take the deer, and got away yourself. A cougar is nothing to mess with."

"I know that," said Martinette impatiently, "but I wasn't going to let it eat Bambi."

"I had a dog once," said another man. "I knew there was a cougar around and I thought the dog would keep it off. But damn, if that dog didn't come running to me for protection the minute we saw the brute."

"A dog is no match for a cougar," said somebody else.

"Well what then?" said the first man. "Did you fight it off with your boat hook?"

"No, John came running up the hill with a stick, and a couple of tourists started screaming and yelling, and it backed off. It ran off into the woods there, toward Potters' place."

"You were lucky. It could have been a lot worse."

"It sure could have. Can you imagine if it had been one of our guests? And you all stand talking while that cougar could be anywhere. I thought you were planning to hunt it down."

"It would help if we had an idea where to look," said one of them.

"It was over at the school yard this morning," I said.

"We better get in touch with Sammy, find out if he's seen it." The loggers all left the store and spread out through the woods toward the Potters' homestead.

"I won't be able to let the kids outside to play until they catch it," I observed.

"A cougar sighting won't do any harm," said Martinette, "but if anybody's killed, that would be bad for business."

"I guess so," I agreed as I picked up my mail. Bad for business? I guess we all have our priorities.

#

For the rest of that day we stayed inside. Richard turned off the generator before it got dark. Usually we left it on until bedtime, but we weren't going to risk having anyone go outside the trailer at night time. We made do with candles and a propane lantern.

I wasn't too worried about Richard and me, but cougars have been known to stalk even adult humans on the Northwest Coast, and they have killed children. We both met our students at the jetty the next morning, waiting for Rainbow and Geoff to bring their two girls. Then Geoff and Pierre walked us all back to the school.

Later that day Rainbow came up to the school, beaming.

"I thought you'd want to hear the news," she exclaimed. "Mr. Edenshaw shot the cougar this morning, up behind your house, Patsy." The Edenshaws lived in a floathouse just a couple of kilometers west of Blubber Bay. Patsy looked proud and pleased.

Rainbow continued. "Your dad came over not long ago. He's going to give me the teeth and claws to make jewelry with. He says he'll share the meat with anybody who wants it."

"Cougar meat? People eat that?" I asked.

"Sure," Rainbow said. "It's good."

"We've had it before," said the Campbell twins.

"I'll bring you some next time we get any," Garth promised.

"Uh, thanks." I'd had the notion that the meat of a predator wasn't all that safe for humans to eat, but it appeared I was wrong. Of course, people ate bear meat, and bears are predators too.

A few days later Garth made good on his promise. The Campbells had gotten a haunch of cougar meat from the Edenshaws and roasted it for dinner. The children brought strips of the cold roast in their lunches the next day.

I tried it gingerly, as did Richard. Donna refused to touch it. It tasted like very dry roast beef.

"Quite delicious," Richard said.

#

Not long after that I was over at the resort one day when a boat came in from the logging camp with a dead cougar tied onto the bow. I'd seen moose and deer tied onto pickup trucks while teaching in other small communities, but this was something a bit different.

I was amazed at the frightful power that these animals show even in death. The thick, flat skull, huge teeth, and solid musculature took my breath away. Dead, the cougar scared me. Alive, it would be truly awesome and terrifying.

Chapter Sixteen

Logging, Fishing and Whaling

We hadn't been back in Blubber Bay long when Nancy arrived for a visit. She seemed a little subdued.

"How did your garden work out?" I asked. I had seen a small patch not far from Rainbow's vegetable garden that I suspected might be Nancy's work.

"Not too well. It rained all summer. Everything I planted went moldy and rotten."

"That's too bad."

"But I grew some chives and parsley in the house. Rainbow gave me seeds."

"And how has the foraging been going?"

"Nothing seems to grow around here. I looked for all the things that were in my books. But except for a few berries I could hardly find a thing to eat."

"So what have you been doing for food?" I asked.

"Ma Potter gave me a bag of flour and some apples and chick peas, and Rainbow gave me a jar of popcorn. And my mother sent me some money to buy stuff."

"You didn't spend it all at Martinette's store, did you?" I asked in alarm.

"No, stuff is way too expensive there. Sammy took me shopping with them in his boat."

"That's good." I tried to think what I could offer a vegan to eat. It sounded like her diet had been pretty limited.

"Would you like a peanut butter sandwich?"

"That would be great."

I put peanut butter and bread on the table, as well as a few apples and bananas that we had brought in with us. Donna and Richard joined us and made sandwiches for themselves while I put water on for tea.

"Do you have any pepper?" Nancy asked. I handed her the shaker. After slicing an apple over the peanut butter on her open face sandwich, Nancy sprinkled the whole thing until it was black.

"What are you doing?" Donna asked, looking horrified.

"Pepper cleans the blood and opens the pores," Nancy explained. "You should try it."

"No thanks." Donna carried her sandwich into the livingroom.

"I can hardly wait to start working in the school again." Nancy took a big bite of her sandwich.

"Uh, well Nancy, Richard and I pretty much have the job covered," I said. "It might not be such a good idea this early in the school year."

"But I love to volunteer! What is it with people around here? Nobody seems to want my help."

"Perhaps it's because you're not very experienced," I suggested.

"I don't think anybody likes me. I've tried really hard to be friendly, you know? And it's so lonely all by myself in that floathouse. I don't know how Grandpa Neils could stand it."

Richard tried to explain. "There are really only two reasons why anyone moves up here; either to make money or because they want to be left alone."

"But money is crass! It's the root of all capitalistic exploitation. I thought people would be more close to nature in a place like this. But everybody's so stand-offish."

"Money can be pretty useful," I said. "Richard's right. People have to keep their distance. You can get to know your neighbors way too well in a small place like this."

Nancy chewed on her sandwich for a while.

"Couldn't I at least come up at recess sometimes? You know, pal around with the kids, help organize some games and stuff."

I wanted to say 'No,' but I couldn't be that mean.

"Just at recess then. Maybe once or twice a week."

"All right! Kids love me. It'll be great, you'll see. I have so many great ideas, don't get me started."

Nancy finished her sandwich, and I gave her the jar of peanut butter to take home.

"Remember," I said. "Just for recess. And not more than two days a week!"

#

As Richard had said, there were basically two kinds of people living around Blubber Bay. Some were there to work, like the loggers and fishermen, and others like Giselle Baker were there to escape.

The Potters and the Goodman family were fishermen. They would turn their hands to logging occasionally, but both Sammy and George owned big fishing boats and took out commercial fishing licenses every year. But Sammy said that their days were numbered. There weren't as many fish as there had been ten or twenty years earlier, and more and more fishermen were having trouble catching enough to cover their expenses.

There were many reasons for this, ranging from over-fishing and poor conservation practices to spraying the areas around spawning streams with pesticides and DDT. Logging ruined other spawning streams. Even in places where fish hatcheries had been introduced, imported species with poor resistance to disease were edging out the native varieties.

George told us about one local fisherman who had rented a refrigerated truck to drive his catch down to town. The cooling unit broke down, ruining his whole payload. The insurance didn't cover the rotting fish, and he lost his fishing boat as a result.

Fishing was not only risky, it could be dangerous as well. George's missing fingers were a reminder of that.

"Take ol' Sam there," said George. "It's rare to see a fisherman with all his fingers. What happens, see, is you've got your hand on the gunwale of the boat. The fishing line goes across your hand. Then suddenly there's a swell, the boat bucks, and kazam . . . no more fingers!"

#

The logging camp children were noticeably more materialistic than the Indians or the floathouse children, and no wonder. A sixteen-year-old drop out could earn more in a year of logging than I did as a teacher. But logging was a dangerous job too.

Garth told the story of a neighbor of theirs who'd been cutting trees by himself. He had a whistle around his neck so that he could blow it in case of a broken leg or other trouble. But a huge limb had fallen on his head, crushing his jaw. Unable to whistle for help, he had walked out of the bush alone, back to the road and the crew foreman.

Although there was no doctor in the area, the foremen had training in first aid, and they often needed it for logging injuries. But that didn't deter young men from signing on. The money was a powerful incentive.

The Potts were a good example. It was no hardship for them to buy a speedboat for their spoiled ten-year-old daughter when Stephanie was causing trouble on Pierre's school boat. The logging camp families could afford to buy whatever they wanted.

The loggers spent their money freely at Martinette's store, unlike the artists, Indians and hippies who preferred to shop in Alert Bay or Port McNeill. The logging camp children would often come to school with money in their pockets, or with candy bars and other treats that they had bought at the resort across the bay. They would laugh scornfully and disbelievingly at any suggestion that not all people could afford such luxuries.

It was different for the floathouse families, many of whom lived hand-to-mouth. Their ideals of simplicity and conservation were incomprehensible to the logging children.

#

Blubber Bay had come by its name honestly. Long ago, whalers had hunted in these waters. The wide, flat shell beach had been a handy place to haul up the big animals and render their fat for sale down south. Nowadays the whalers were long gone. They had been replaced by whale watchers.

Occasionally Geoff or Pierre would attempt to make some extra money by taking out a few of Martinette's tourists to look for a local pod of killer whales. Although the whales traveled long distances, there was a pretty good chance of finding them in certain favorite spots.

We had seen the whales just once, on one of our trips to Port McNeill. Five adults and two young ones were "spy hopping". With their heads and upper bodies out of the water they balanced upright in a row, as if watching to see what was passing by on top of their ocean world.

It was much more common to see seals. As curious as household pets they would swim alongside our boat, looking like dogs eager to go for a walk. The seals were friendly and would come within a couple meters of the trimaran, often accompanying us for several kilometers before going off on business of their own.

#

Mrs. Potts came to see me one day in October, bringing Mrs. Campbell along for support. She was angry.

I had met Stephanie and Helen's mother only briefly at our school play and Track-and-Field event the year before. I'd never had the chance to really talk to her, but I remembered that Mrs. Potts shared Helen's pasty complexion and dumpy physique.

"Stephanie tells me you only gave her a 'C'," she fumed.

"A 'C'?"

"In her research project!"

"Oh." The senior students had been assigned to research an animal of their choice the month before. We had practiced research skills in class, and I had reminded them of the steps they should be following throughout the month of the assignment.

"She worked all day on that project! And you only gave her a 'C'."

"I didn't *give* her the 'C'," I said. "She *earned* the 'C'. Helen got a 'B' on hers, didn't she?"

"What does Helen's mark matter? Stephanie should have a 'B' at least. She worked so hard on it, she deserves an 'A'."

"But they were supposed to spend a whole month on their project. You said that Stephanie only spent a day on hers."

"She worked very hard."

Mrs. Campbell looked indignant too, but she couldn't really complain. Her girls had all gotten 'B's on their projects, and Garth had taken home an 'A'."

I refused to change Stephanie's mark, and Mrs. Potts stormed away even angrier than when she had arrived. It seemed that a job in diplomacy would probably never be a good career choice for me.

Chapter Seventeen

Principal Visits

Professional development days are important for teachers, but especially for those who work in small and isolated schools. It gives a chance to update skills, to hear about the latest research and innovations, and to talk with other teachers about techniques for dealing with common problems.

I looked forward to my professional days. Three times a year workshops were held in Port McNeill, and Frank Weston arranged every time for a float plane to pick me up.

Although I enjoyed the freedom and autonomy of Blubber Bay School, the professional isolation could be difficult. That's why I'd found the lack of rapport with Mercy so disappointing. It's hard to stay inspired in a vacuum, although I was lucky that Frank tried hard to respond to all my needs, and I did have Richard to talk to about our students.

On my first professional day in Blubber Bay I was very excited. It was late November, and I hadn't been "to town" for months. I could hardly wait to spend the day in a big school and rub shoulders with other teachers.

A fine drizzle was falling as I walked down to the jetty in my good clothes, and I wondered if I should have brought an umbrella. The plane was supposed to pick me up at 8 a.m., but I didn't know how long I'd really have to wait.

An hour later the drizzle had increased to a downpour, and I

128

was definitely wishing I'd brought the umbrella. I sloshed my way back up to the school, and got on the radio phone.

"You'd better get back down to the dock," Frank said. "The plane should be there any minute."

So down I trudged again, this time better protected against the rain. Two hours later I was on the phone again.

It took a while for Frank to report back.

"The planes couldn't fly," he said. "The weather's too bad. Sorry."

After that I learned not to go down to the dock until I could hear a plane approaching. Even at that, I missed most of the workshops offered in the two years I was there. One P.D. day the plane did come, but not until 11 a.m. By the time I arrived at North Island Secondary School the catered buffet lunch was being cleared away, and I was only able to attend one afternoon seminar.

Sometimes Frank would make a principal's visit to Blubber Bay School. These were major events for us. The kids would prepare their best work to show him, or plan a recitation or some other special event. Every once in a while a Special Education consultant, Union representative, or the janitorial supervisor would come with him.

The visits usually went well, although mishaps did occur. One day the kids were enjoying an extended recess while Frank and I talked, when suddenly several children burst into the classroom exclaiming, "Mrs. Todd! Laverne's finger is caught in the fence!" Laverne had thrust her finger through a link of chain, and she was quite unable to remove it. She giggled as we discussed the best way to extract her finger, deciding that amputation was the only answer. But after I sent Donna to fetch some margarine from the teacherage, Laverne's finger slipped out quite easily.

All too often a scheduled visit would have to be cancelled partway through the morning due to unsafe flying weather. This was always a let-down for the students as well as for me.

Frank was adamant that I should not give in to pressure from parents like Giselle, Mrs. Campbell, or Mrs. Potts. His advice helped me to keep my perspective as our situation grew slowly worse.

#

Nancy discovered that by bringing her lunch on fine days when we were eating outside, she could extend her time in the playground quite a bit longer than the fifteen-minute morning recess. She usually brought home-made chapatis and humus, liberally sprinkled with pepper. The first time the kids saw it, several of them gagged. None of them wanted to sit beside her because of the pepper and her garlicky smell.

Sometimes for variety Nancy would make herself a pita sandwich with peanut butter, brewer's yeast and sprouts. While they were eating, the kids would discuss their lunches with a broad emphasis on meat products that I found much too funny to put a stop to.

"Yum! Cougar steak!" Lindsay Campbell would say, holding up a piece of cold meat. "Want some, Nancy?"

"I have a ham sandwich!" Stephanie would gloat.

Even Summer Sunshine couldn't resist. "We're having clam bake for supper tonight."

"We had clam chowder last night," Patsy Edenshaw would say. She loved clam chowder.

"My dad is going deer hunting on the weekend. He says I can go with him."

"No fair, Garth," one of the twins would protest. "You went last time."

Sometimes for variety the logging kids would talk about Dairy Queen, Burger King, or other favorite fast food joints that they visited in town. The Hurley and Davidson children had never been to these places and were wildly interested and envious.

"MacDonald's is the best," the Campbell children agreed. "We saw Ronald MacDonald in Campbell River one time. He was blowing up balloons and giving them out."

"Mine popped," little Davy said sadly.

"I love their hamburgers."

"Mmmmm!"

Nancy could take only so much of this. "MacDonald's exploits the planet!" she would exclaim. "Don't you remember that I told you their beef comes from South America? The Brazilian rain forests, the lungs of the Earth, are being cut down so that MacDonald's can provide those hamburgers, you know."

"Mmmmm!" the kids would repeat, with ill-concealed grins.

#

It was easy to pull Nancy's leg. Hans was an expert.

Our lumpy and irregular playground required modifications to the rules of almost any game. Not only was running awkward since you had to watch your feet at all times, but we lost balls almost daily either into the bush on one side or into the bay on the other.

The other children were reluctant to play with Hans by this time as he'd become quite bossy and aggressive, so Nancy agreed to engage him in a game of "one on one." Hans was charming and appreciative as he suggested a game of soccer, using pylons to mark the goals.

Soon Nancy and Hans were racing up and down the school yard while the rest of the students either watched or played their own games. Nancy was soon huffing and puffing, but too intent on the game to notice what was obvious to the rest of us.

Hans had no trouble cornering the ball, and with a well-aimed kick he sent it, not toward the goal post, but into the "chuck."

"You'll have to get it," he told Nancy. "That's the rules of the game."

Nancy took off her sandals and rolled up her flowered overalls. She waded after the ball with a stick, but by the time she got back with it she was muddy and soaked.

Hans was full of concern, but assured Nancy that it was the best time he'd had in ages.

"Nobody will play with me here," he said. "I've been so lonely."

"I know what it feels like," Nancy said. "I'll be glad to play with you Hans, any time you want."

Nancy continued to wade after the ball twice a week until the weather got cold enough that I decided to put a stop to it. I was afraid that she'd catch pneumonia.

"Hans is such a nice boy," Nancy told me. "He just needs somebody to pay attention to him. I told you the kids would love having me around."

#

In November there was a teachers' strike. This put me in a very difficult position. On the one hand I didn't want to be a union "scab", but on the other hand I really couldn't see going on strike in Blubber Bay.

For one thing, there was no way of knowing how long it would last. We would go stir crazy with nothing to do. We needed the income, but even more we needed the structure and routine that teaching school gave us.

Our students needed it even more. Their parents would be justifiably angry if we forced their children to stay home, unable even to play outside because of the rain. School was the only chance these kids had for a social life.

And what if I did go on strike? Quite apart from becoming a community pariah, it would be just too absurd to march up and down our jetty with a union placard.

Finally a solution revealed itself. Our radio phone was an unreliable instrument. Poor weather conditions often produced static that made communication impossible for days on end. This could be extremely frustrating when I needed Frank's help with a problem.

But now it worked in our favor. Amazingly, our radio phone did not work during the days leading up to the strike. If the union was making any demands, it was impossible for me to know what they were. I could continue teaching with a clear conscience.

Richard came home from a visit with Martinette a few days later to report that the teacher's strike was over. It had lasted only three days. And the next day our phone mysteriously started working again.

#

Frank Weston called in early December to say that he'd be over the following day. Complaints had been phoned in to the Board office in Port Hardy, so Frank had been instructed to meet with the unhappy parents and get to the root of the problem.

"Who phoned?" I asked. "What were they complaining about?"

"I'll know more when I see you tomorrow." The radio phone was crackling and cutting out, so there was no point trying to discuss it then.

The following day Frank arrived in mid-morning. A public meeting had been called for noon.

"Can you look after the students outside while we meet in the classroom?" Frank asked Richard. Fortunately the weather was pretty good.

I was feeling too tense and nervous to teach well. Frank had told me that Mrs. Campbell and Mrs. Potts had phoned the School Board with complaints, but that he was expecting a number of other parents as well.

By lunchtime we could see a group of parents straggling up the hill, so Richard bundled up the class and they went out into the yard. I couldn't eat, and Frank said that he wasn't hungry either.

Soon Mrs. Campbell, Mrs. Potts, Giselle Baker, Charlotte Hill, and Pierre were seated on the tiny chairs around our work table. Charlotte and Pierre smiled and said Hello as they came in, but the other three women looked angry. They sat stiffly on the chairs that Frank indicated and wouldn't look at me.

"Mrs. Campbell, Mrs. Potts, I understand you have some concerns," Frank said.

Mrs. Campbell seemed to be their spokeswoman. "We certainly do. The Todds are not working out at all. Mrs. Todd doesn't know how to teach. She told Lisa the other day that she's fat. And Mr. Todd can't keep his hands off the girls. Laverne has told me how he looks down her blouse."

"What? That's so untrue!" I exclaimed.

Frank raised his hand slightly, as if to tell me that he'd handle this.

"Why does Lisa say that Mrs. Todd called her fat?"

"The twins told me. And they told me how he looks at them," said Mrs. Campbell, staring through the window at the back of Richard's head as he watched the children play.

"The twins. They're the ones wearing the skimpy halters, aren't they?"

"Yeah. What of it?"

"It's December," said Frank. "Winter time. Even in summer, halters would not be appropriate for school. I'd appreciate it if you'd make sure that your girls are properly covered up from now on."

Mrs. Campbell's face darkened. "What about that Sex Education? That's not a proper subject for children this age."

"Didn't you sign a permission slip for your children to take that course?"

"Well yes, but . . ."

Frank turned to me. "Mrs. Todd, did any parents refuse to give permission?"

"Yes," I said. "Pierre's son Sylvain was excused from those classes."

"Did Mrs. Todd teach your children anything untrue or inappropriate?"

"She did tell Stephanie in front of all the other children that her mother here was wrong about what she had told her girls," Mrs. Campbell replied. "Made her feel real stupid."

In response to Frank's raised eyebrows I repeated the conversation we'd had months ago about how boys and girls are made. "Perhaps Stephanie misunderstood her mother," I said.

"Perhaps. Mrs. Potts, what do you say?"

"That teacher gives my girl bad marks. Stephanie is bright, she's hard working. But she can't follow the lessons. They're too hard."

Frank picked up the class register and perused attendance for the year so far.

"I see that Stephanie and Helen have been absent almost one third of the time since school started. Why is that?"

"They're here a lot. Sometimes the boat won't start. What's that got to do with it?"

"It's not surprising that your daughter is having difficulty if she's not attending school regularly," Frank pointed out. "Pierre's boat always starts. Perhaps the girls should resume using the school boat."

Before Mrs. Potts could reply, Frank turned to the other three parents.

"None of you phoned the School Board, yet I see that you have concerns."

"I'm not worried about education in the school," said Pierre. "I just came because I want to know what's going on. I would like to mention that the twins have been tormenting Lisa on the boat ride home. I've tried to stop them, but they don't listen to me. Maybe Mrs. Campbell could talk to them."

Mrs. Campbell gave Pierre a very nasty look. "You don't need to tell me how to bring up my own children."

"Mrs. Baker, what about you?" Frank asked.

"I'm not pleased with the school. I've made that plain. Hans is not appreciated or challenged here. The teacher picks on him because he's smarter than all the other kids."

"So the lessons are too easy?"

Giselle nodded.

"And Mrs. Potts, you say the lessons are too hard?"

Mrs. Potts looked a little confused.

"Have either of you read through the British Columbia Elementary Curriculum guide? Are you familiar with standardized assessment procedures?"

"I know what's right for my son," Giselle insisted.

"That's good. And I think we'll have to accept that Mrs. Todd knows what is right for her class. Mrs. Todd, how long did you go to university?"

"Five years," I said.

"You studied Education at university for five years?"

"Yes."

"Mmm hmm. Mrs. Hill, I've been told you were a most effective teacher's aide. During your months of working at the school, what was your impression of Mrs. Todd's teaching?"

"Oh, she's a good teacher," said Charlotte. "Sometimes a little rough and ready with the kids perhaps, but she has a good program in place."

"Thank you," said Frank. "Is there anything else?"

Mrs. Campbell and Mrs. Potts were not appeased. They would clearly have liked to say more, but Frank stood and showed them to the door.

"Thank you so much for coming in. We're lucky to have a teacher like Mrs. Todd in Blubber Bay."

He shook hands warmly with Pierre and chatted with him for a few minutes, then went to join Richard in the playground while I collected my nerves. I was surprised yet pleased that Charlotte had put in a good word for me. Perhaps Martinette's warnings were without foundation. I could only hope so, since there was sure to be trouble in the months ahead regardless of Charlotte's input.

A supportive principal is beyond all price, yet it was still a long afternoon. I was glad when it was time to walk the children down to their boats.

#

This was one of the occasions when Sylvia and George were away in town, so I knew that Mercy would be coming to clean the school. I was eager to talk to her about the meeting we'd had, and to find out whether she'd experienced anything similar during her days as the Blubber Bay teacher.

It turned out that Mercy already knew all about the meeting. "Mrs. Campbell and Mrs. Potts came to see me after they left here," she said.

"Did they ask you to apply for the teaching job?"

"I told them I wasn't interested. But they like my methods. And I do understand the community, after all."

"I wish you'd been here this afternoon."

"I don't come to school meetings. I know what goes on in a school."

"But your perspective might have been really helpful. After all, you are the only mother around here who knows what it's like to be a teacher."

"You can't have two teachers in a classroom."

Mercy seemed pleased, but I wasn't sure why. Was it because of the compliments she had received from her two visitors? I had hoped for reassurance, but my conversation with Mercy left me feeling even more uneasy.

Frank had won a battle, but we had still to fight the war.

Chapter Eighteen

Christmas

With Christmas approaching, Richard and I decided that it would be fun to spend the holiday in Blubber Bay. The previous year Donna and I had flown out as soon as school finished in December. This year they were calling for snow, and the weather did not look promising either to fly out or to take the boat down to Victoria.

We did go for a two-day visit to Port McNeill to shop in town, and my mother mailed up a parcel of gifts for Donna. Given the number of conifers that grew behind the school we were sure that we could find a suitable Christmas tree.

Best of all, once the Potters heard that we were planning to stay in the area, they invited us for Christmas dinner along with the Goodmans, the Hurleys, and Reverend Smith and his wife.

#

On Christmas morning Donna knew better than to get up too early since we'd have no light or heat until Richard traipsed outside to turn on the generator. But eventually we were all up and opening presents by the tree. Donna was especially excited about a Michael Jackson tape that my mother had sent up; he was her favorite singer that year.

I made pancakes for breakfast, then Donna went down to the

138

Hurley floathouse to show Summer Sunshine her new tape. Soon she was back, and none too soon for it had started to snow. The large soft flakes melted as soon as they hit the ground, but they'd make the wooden ramp dangerously slippery.

Early in the afternoon we got ready to walk to the Potters'. As always, we had to be aware of the level of the tide when crossing the mud flats at the head of the bay. With gumboots on our feet we carried our shoes in a bag, Richard's backpack stuffed with a tin of cookies and a bag of fruit from Port McNeill to contribute to the feast.

The snow fell steadily, and was starting to stick to the ground now. Donna was fascinated by it as we hadn't seen snow at all the year before. She ran ahead of us, hopping and using a stick to make curious tracks along the path.

Smoke from a wood fire puffed from the chimney of Emmy and Andy's house as we passed it. In front of Sammy's house we could see his fishing boat tied up to their dock, and across from it the Goodman's large boat. The small run-about that Ma and Granny shared was pulled up in front of Granny's floathouse. The Hurleys were just rounding the point and heading into Potter Cove in their small motor boat.

Richard went to catch their lines and help Geoff tie up their boat while Donna and I went into the house. Reverend and Marjorie Smith were already there. When I remarked that I hadn't seen their boat, Mrs. Smith explained that they were staying for a few days with the Goodmans, and had come over with them.

The Potter home had been designed with a lot of company in mind. The living room was spacious, with a high, beamed ceiling. Besides the masks and candy jars, an accumulation of small paintings, driftwood, and petit point tapestries decorated the walls. The dining area and living room overlooked Potter Cove, where Granny's house and a variety of floating sheds were tucked into the curve of the bay off to our right.

A wooden crate loosely covered with a blanket peeped intriguingly from behind the heavy black wood stove. In front of the wood stove a pair of wet boots were turned upside down on a rack.

"What's in the crate?" I asked.

"Paddy's chicks," said Sammy. She thinks with this snow it's too cold for them outside."

Sylvia and Mercy Goodman were in the kitchen helping Ma and Emmy prepare the meal, so I dropped off our bag of food and joined the group in the livingroom. Andy was relaxing in a cavernous armchair with Mrs. Smith and Granny perched on either side, gazing at the newborn infant nestled in the crook of Andy's elbow. Emmy had given birth the month before to their first son, with just Andy and Ma in attendance.

"Help yourself kids," Sammy said as he proffered jars of candy. Donna, Wilson and Bobby took large handfuls then started crawling behind the furniture, chasing a litter of kittens that was hiding under the couch.

George bellowed with laughter. "A candy a day keeps the dentist away, eh Sam? Where's Paddy?"

"Out looking after those damn chinchillas. Those animals are more trouble than they're worth, I'm telling ya."

I went over to admire the baby as Richard came in with the Hurleys. Rainbow joined the women in the overcrowded kitchen for a while, then made a tour of the living room with a tray of crackers topped with crab and shrimp salad.

Reverend Smith and I eventually ended up on the couch with an assortment of kittens and kids crawling around our feet.

"This reminds me of the first Christmas that Mrs. Smith and I were married," he reminisced with a smile.

"It was in the Alaskan panhandle in 1944, not far north of the Queen Charlotte Islands. We tied up at a small public dock and after supper went up to shore to stretch our legs. There were a couple of abandoned buildings, still in good repair, and one inhabited house. We stopped in and they not only invited us for tea, but asked us to come back the following day for Christmas supper.

"The next day the weather blew in cold. Mid-way through the morning another boat came in, a small one. A man came out and tied up his vessel, then he went below. He didn't seem to want to talk or visit, so we left them alone.

"It was a pretty spot. At one time it must have been a tidy little farm. There was still an orchard, and a solitary cow who was glad to have our company.

"Finally the man emerged from his boat and approached my wife. Mrs. Smith was very young back then, but she had a way about her, you could tell she would help anybody. He said that his wife had just given birth, and as another woman, would she come and help.

"Mrs. Smith did what she could, then I was invited on board and we baptized the baby. Alexander I remember his name was. A little boy, born on Christmas Day."

"That's a pretty amazing coincidence," I said, smiling.

Reverend Smith nodded. "Our Lord was born in a stable, just as young Alexander was born on a fishing boat. It struck me that we'd been given a sign, to strengthen us in our calling."

"It was something you could think about during those years of missionary work."

"It helped us get through some difficult times," Reverend Smith admitted.

"Ollie and Lilly Hochstetter lived in the house, and when they heard that a baby had just been born down at their dock, they couldn't do enough for the couple. When we left a day later, Alexander and his parents were in good hands."

#

Finally supper was laid out on the huge table that Sammy had built from hand-hewn cedar planks years before, and Ma called us all to "Set and eat." Granny went to the door and shooed the dogs and Morris outside, then shrieked to Paddy that supper was on.

Ma and Sammy sat in chairs at the two ends of the table, but most of the rest of us sat on benches along the sides. Granny and Mrs. Smith had chairs too as the ends of the table were easily wide enough to accommodate two people. Mrs. Smith wanted to give her chair to Emmy, who was now holding the baby, but Emmy refused.

"He'll be ready for his nap soon. You just stay put."

We could hear Paddy stomping mud off her feet as she came in and kicked off her boots. A moment later she slid onto the end of the bench near Sammy's chair.

"Looks like we're all here now," said Ma.

Reverend Smith bowed his head. "May the Lord make us truly grateful for the good food He has set upon this table." Sylvia and Mrs. Smith quickly bowed their heads too, while Mercy and Rainbow hushed the children.

"God didn't put this food on the table, my father and mother did," said Paddy.

Ma Potter and George Goodman laughed while Mercy observed, "Isn't that *funny?*"

Reverend Smith laughed too.

We all reached for what was nearest and spent the next several minutes passing dishes and serving ourselves from platters of turkey, roast fish, crab casserole, bread stuffing, squash, cooked carrots, lima beans, mashed potatoes, and yams. Geoff and Rainbow had brought over home-made root beer, knowing there'd be nothing stronger served in the Potter house.

Mercy handed out festive Christmas crackers that she had made herself, complete with exploding ends to tug on, small prizes and party hats. Everybody laughed when George placed a pale blue bonnet on his head. Soon Granny was topped by a yellow paper crown and even the dignified Smiths had paper hats sitting askew on their heads.

Donna blew on a whistle that had fallen out of her Christmas cracker, and I threatened to take it away from her. No sooner was I over-ruled by the other adults at the table when Wilson held up a handful of snapping paper strips left over from his mother's cracker-making session.

"So that's where those got to," Mercy said as Wilson shared out the strips with the other children and they took turns seeing who could make the loudest bang.

We ate steadily for close to an hour. Morris turned up on the window sill outside and meowed to be let in.

"I'm starving out here!" Sammy complained in the cat's voice. "Somebody let me in!"

After supper the women took turns washing dishes, then Ma and Emmy served dessert. Besides a flaming Christmas pudding with hard sauce there were cookies, apple and pumpkin pie, a fruit cake, and apple strudel. We were all too stuffed to eat much, but Ma said that we could come back to it later.

"Everybody sit in the livingroom!" Sylvia called out. She clapped her hands for attention. "We're going to play some games now!"

The women and children sat down eagerly. Geoff and Andy scuffed their feet and looked around furtively as if they'd rather be somewhere else. I noticed that the baby had woken from his nap and Richard had cleverly managed to take the infant from Emmy. He enjoyed dandling babies, so he'd be able to avoid the games if they got too silly.

"First we'll play Adjective Story." Sylvia handed out a small piece of paper and a pencil to each person. "Everybody write three adjectives on their paper. Boys, Autumn Mist, if you need any help you just ask one of the grown-ups."

We all wrote our adjectives, then Sylvia read aloud a long, rollicking story with lots of blank spaces for us to fill in.

"And now, Red Bloomers!" Sylvia held up a large, neatly wrapped box. "There is a pair of red bloomers in this box. We hand it around the circle, and everybody takes off one layer of paper when it gets to them. Whoever takes off the last layer of paper has to open the box and put on the red bloomers."

Most of the adults groaned, and the Smiths smiled broadly although we could see that they were hoping very much not to get the bloomers. Richard made it clear that he was absorbed in the baby and wouldn't be able to play the game.

Red bloomers! As the layers of paper came off the box, each face became more and more anxious in turn. Donna and Wilson were disappointed that they *didn't* get the bloomers, but most of the adults couldn't hide their relief. Geoff and Andy in particular were clearly making heroic struggles to be good sports.

Finally Granny gave a scream as she realized she was taking off the final layer of wrapping paper. She opened the box slowly . . . and took out a corsage made of two beautiful rose buds!

We played a few other games, then moved the furniture out of the way so we could dance. Sammy set up a portable record player while George showed us how to do the schottische.

"One two three hop, step hop, step hop," he chanted as he danced across the living room with Sylvia's hand held in his. George was surprisingly light on his feet for a big man, and Sylvia was as graceful as ever.

Donna and I danced together since Richard was still busy with the baby, and Wilson danced with his mother. There wasn't room for everybody to dance at the same time so we had to take turns.

After the schottische, which takes a lot of room, George announced that we would try a few square dances. That way eight people could dance at a time.

"Don't worry if you've never done this before. Sylvia and I will teach you."

George and Sylvia demonstrated the basic steps, and since most of us had square danced before, we were soon ready to start.

"Now the fiddler's ready, let us all begin, so step it out and step it in!"

Emmy took the baby to nurse and Richard joined a set as my partner.

"Do-si-do and swing your gal! Gentlemen, bow to the lady on your right!"

After a few square dances we tried a reel, then we were all ready to take a break and eat more desserts. It had been dark for hours by now, and Rainbow regretfully announced that they would have to take the girls home to bed.

"No Mom, no!" they protested. But Geoff and Rainbow bundled them into coats and boots, while Andy offered to see them down to the dock.

Richard and Donna and I got ready to head home too. The wet snow still fell out of a calm sky, ankle deep by now. Christmas lights outlined the Potter's house, and phosphorescence in the water gave the scene an other-worldly glow. We could hear Autumn Mist wailing loudly with exhaustion as Geoff started their engine and puttered away.

The light was bright on the snow as we walked home. We could hear the generator over at the resort humming in a friendly and restful way. The air smelled very clean. All was peaceful and right with the world!

Chapter Nineteen

Bitter Lessons

The day after Christmas Donna built a snowman laced with grass and mud. The snow melted the day after that, and our usual rainy weather resumed.

We had an unexpected visit a few days after Christmas. Giselle Baker came by with Hans.

Rod had dropped by occasionally until he'd moved away, but we'd never had a social visit from Giselle. When we saw her in passing over at the resort we hadn't talked. Richard was a little afraid of being misunderstood, and Giselle always seemed to be leaving just as I was arriving.

Donna invited Hans to join her in a game of Scrabble and they set up the board at the kitchen table while we adults sat in the living room. Donna had really liked Hans the first year we lived in Blubber Bay. He was good looking and intelligent, and since he had lived in Vancouver until he was nine years old he was more cosmopolitan than the other children at our school.

But Hans had changed over the past few months. He was becoming defiant and wilful, but always in a subtle way that was difficult to confront and discipline. Since he was the eldest boy in the school, apart from good-natured Patrick, he was able to dominate many of the younger children. Recess play had become more aggressive, and often ended in tears or angry words.

Richard and I had caught Hans in a few minor lies as well. He would sometimes deny doing things that we were quite certain he had done. He was becoming sneaky and manipulative. Or perhaps he had always been that way and we just hadn't seen it before.

Giselle seemed edgy and defensive, but that wasn't surprising. She refused my offer of tea. Was she afraid we might poison her?

"Hans tells me you've been picking on him," she said.

"No, we wouldn't do that," I replied. "Hans is a fine boy, but he has been acting up a bit lately. Perhaps he's unhappy since Rod left."

Giselle stiffened. "I kicked him out. Rod was trying to come between Hans and me."

After a quick glance at me, Richard got up and went to Donna and Hans at the kitchen table. "Time to play outside, kids."

"But it's wet outside," Donna protested.

"You can put on your boots. Play hide-and-seek or something in the playground for a few minutes, okay?"

Reluctantly they complied, and Richard rejoined us in the livingroom.

"Hans and I have always been very close," Giselle continued. "I moved up here to get him away from bad influences."

"You used to live in Vancouver, didn't you?" I said.

"Yes, I grew up there. But the schools there never understood him, and I didn't like the other children he was exposed to."

"Does your family live in Vancouver?" Richard asked. "You and Hans must miss them."

"I don't want anything to do with my family. They were trying to wean Hans's affections away from me. I've forbidden them to have anything to do with us."

"Hans must feel very cut off from other people," Richard suggested.

"He has me. We're very close. He tells me all the time that we're best friends."

I didn't know what to say, but Giselle continued.

"This school is not meeting Hans's needs. He is a top athlete.

He's a very gifted student, very artistic. You're really not doing anything to develop his talents."

"I agree, he is a talented boy," I said, "but we have a very large class for a one-room school. Hans is actually lucky that he's in a grade with several other children. Most of the lessons and activities are geared for his level."

"You're not challenging him. Hans tells me that none of the other children come close to him."

"Well, I wouldn't say that. Sylvain and Summer Sunshine are extremely bright, and Wilson is a very talented artist. But Hans has become quite uncooperative lately. I can see that he is unhappy, but he doesn't seem willing to meet us halfway."

"Wilson!" Giselle snorted. "He can't even read. And the other two are younger than Hans. How are they supposed to challenge him?"

"Maybe Hans would be better off in a bigger school."

"Or correspondence courses might suit you better," Richard suggested.

Giselle pursed her lips as she stood up.

"I see you have no interest in helping me. I came to you in good faith, but it's just as I suspected. You have no interest in providing a good education."

"I'm sorry you feel that way," I replied tartly.

Giselle left without saying goodbye. She called for Hans as she strode toward the jetty, brushing by Donna without a word.

"He kept hiding but he wouldn't play," Donna complained. "Can I go see Summer Sunshine?" I nodded, and she went down to the Hurley's floathouse for the rest of the afternoon while Richard and I discussed our strange visitor.

That night when I tried to cook supper, the stove wouldn't start. The pilot light was out. We soon discovered that the fridge wasn't working either. When Richard investigated, he found that the valves on our two hundred-pound propane tanks had been loosened. All our fuel had leaked away during the afternoon.

Donna insisted that she didn't know anything about it, so we could only assume that Hans had loosened the valves. Had he done it accidentally, through childish curiosity, or was it malicious? We both believed that a boy of Hans's intelligence would have known full well what he was doing.

Richard made a second trip over to the resort, having already made a mail-run that day, and arranged to get our propane tanks refilled.

#

The day after Giselle's visit the weather seemed to be clearing up, so we decided to take the boat to Port McNeill for a couple of days. We were feeling "bushed" and a change of scenery would help a lot, not to mention a restaurant meal and the chance to go shopping.

We motored for the first few hours, then Richard decided it was a good opportunity to sail. The conditions were perfect, with a steady wind blowing from the right direction for once. We hoisted the mainsail and the jib, then I went below to prepare lunch.

Suddenly the boat gave a funny jerk and I could hear a flapping noise, with something banging on the deck.

"The jib shackle has broken!" Richard called down the hatch. "Quick, come up and take the helm."

I climbed the ladder to the cockpit and took the tiller from Richard. He scampered forward, grabbing at the flapping sail and wrestling with it in an effort to get it under control. Suddenly his glasses were whipped off and flew overboard.

"Damn!" Richard lunged for his glasses as the sail smacked him in the face.

He took the jib down and stuffed it through the hatch into the forecastle. Very soberly we sailed on. Apart from the loss of the glasses, we were crossing the southern portion of Queen Charlotte Strait, where hurricane-force winds sweep down from the north with very little warning. Even large, well-equipped vessels had been lost in these waters. Five ships had gone down in a storm the winter before, when Coast Guard warnings did not get through in time.

Our stay in Port McNeill wasn't as much fun as we'd hoped it would be. Richard spent a lot of time trying to replace the broken shackle, and was constantly on the phone to Victoria, arranging to get a new pair of glasses made and shipped up to him.

#

A week later we ran out of oil for the generator. Apparently with all the snow and cold weather over the holidays we had used far more fuel than usual. By then school was back in session, so we were trying to teach without lights, heat, or plumbing.

Bucketing up water from the beach to flush the toilets was not a big problem. The kids were used to doing that, and they enjoyed the break from routine. They mainly complained because the water was so cold. The classroom was cold too. Even with a kerosene heater that Sammy Potter loaned us standing in the middle of the floor, we had to huddle around it with our coats on.

Lessons were a challenge with everyone seated in a circle, trying to squeeze as close to the heater as possible. Notebooks had to be balanced on laps padded with snowpants and heavy jackets. Writing was even more difficult, as half the kids were wearing mitts and the other half had fingers numbed by the cold.

Richard and Donna and I took to sleeping on the boat, as the small interior was easier to heat than the trailer. We still did the cooking and ate our meals in the trailer, bucketing water from the stream behind the school so we could wash our dishes.

It was a great day when the oil barge arrived and refilled our tank. Never since then have we taken electricity for granted.

#

I hadn't seen Nancy Jacobsen since Frank's visit to the school in December, and I started to worry. In truth I didn't *want* to see her, but I would feel horribly guilty if she starved to death or suffered some other mishap. But before my sense of duty forced me to go and invite Nancy for supper, Rainbow told me that she was on an extended visit to Giselle Baker's house.

My look of astonishment prompted her to continue.

"I know, I was as surprised as you. But one day Giselle came over in her boat and stayed for quite a while. When she left she took Nancy with her. They haven't been back since."

"Well, I couldn't be more stunned if you knocked me over with a two-by-four," I said, borrowing a phrase from George Goodman. "I wonder what this means."

I found out what it meant a week or two later, when Nancy turned up for her recess visit. Instead of offering to play with the kids, she wanted to talk to me.

"I have a few suggestions that might improve the school," she said with a big smile.

"That's very nice, Nancy, but I'm an experienced teacher with my program in place. I'm not planning to change anything."

"Oh no, I don't want you to change your program," Nancy assured me. "I just thought that a bit more loving kindness might improve the tone of the school, you know?"

"Loving kindness."

"Yes. Children need love and understanding. Hans tells me that the kids are often not very nice to each other. That comes down from the top, you know."

"Perhaps Hans is the one who needs to start practicing more love and kindness."

Nancy looked at me reproachfully. "Giselle told me you'd say something like that. She's an amazing person."

"She certainly is."

Missing my dry tone, Nancy continued. "Giselle is a vegan too. She's very concerned about the world's problems. And she is a wonderful mother. You might be a little closer to Donna if you'd try some of her methods."

"Thanks, I have marking to do." I moved away, but Nancy followed me into the classroom.

"Giselle told me that it would be hard for you to accept the truth. *There are no eyes so blind as those that will not see.* But I have all kinds of great ideas. We could start with a friendship circle, and teach the kids to hug . . ."

With my hand on her back, I pushed Nancy out the door.

"Sorry, but your services will no longer be required. Please do not come back during school hours any more."

"Giselle said you'd do something like this. Why is it so hard for you to care about other people? Don't worry, I won't give up on you!"

As she walked down the school yard in her wet sandals, I could hear Nancy singing *We Shall Overcome* in a thin, wavering voice.

I steamed as I reported the conversation to Richard.

"A vegan indeed! We've seen Hans eat meat often enough. How dare they try to tell me how to run my school."

But it was true, I had to admit, that the relaxed and happy atmosphere I'd come back to in September had largely evaporated. I'd been ascribing it to the time of the year. The rain and gloom of January were very depressing, and everybody was feeling house-bound and irritable. This volatile "cabin fever" usually came to a head in February, then dissipated slowly as the weather cleared and spring picked up our spirits.

Veronica Hill was becoming more and more surly. Most mornings when I said 'Good Morning' to her she wouldn't even reply. *She's turning into a teenager* I'd thought, but maybe it was more than that.

And Stephanie Potts was more insolent than ever before. Since the meeting in December she seemed to feel that she had a parental sanction to misbehave, and perhaps she did.

The twins and Lisa were becoming more difficult to handle too. In girls their age hormonal changes could cause problems in any classroom, but again their attitudes went beyond what I'd usually expect.

The boys were easier to get along with, except for Hans, but Timothy was becoming more and more withdrawn. He would sit for hours, not talking to anyone and not even pretending to look at his work. I worried about him desperately. He still hadn't been taken for the operation on his legs, and the School Board wasn't able to provide any services to our remote location that might help him. Poor Timothy was left in limbo. He seemed oblivious to Richard and me when we tried to encourage him.

#

About the same time, a plane load of loggers was killed when their chartered plane crashed while taking off from Port Hardy. They were all single men without families, but it was a blow to the kids from the logging camp. The children knew some of the young men who were killed.

Most pilots would not fly if there was any doubt of safety. Fog and high winds were the most common reasons for cancelling a flight. As the sign in the Kelsey Bay office read, "Don't press your pilot. Don't press your luck. Weather can kill!" When Richard saw that he said that he didn't need to be reminded; if his pilot didn't want to fly, he didn't either.

On this occasion it was the owner of the airline who was flying, and unlike most pilots he had a reputation for being rather careless. He had taken off with cold engines and an overloaded plane, and the lives of several people paid for his mistake.

Even at that, I was sometimes surprised at what a good pilot would undertake to deliver. Richard and I were over at the store one day when we heard a plane coming in.

"That must be the new guests I'm expecting," Martinette said, pushing past us and out to the dock. A small Beaver circled around then roared toward the dock, cutting its engines at the last moment. The pilot stepped out onto the pontoon and threw his lines to Richard.

Inside the plane we could hear a dog barking hysterically. A young labrador pressed its nose against the window and slobbered while a fog of cigarette smoke wafted from the open door.

"Looks like you had quite a trip," Richard observed.

"My god, I wondered if we'd make it," the pilot replied. He started handing down duffel bags, suitcases, mailbags, grocery cartons, and a large clothes hamper. I could see three passengers moving inside the plane, then suddenly the dog broke free and leapt onto the dock. Martinette grabbed its collar and petted the dog vigorously while Bambi watched from a safe distance.

"There's a good fellow. Yes, he's a happy boy, isn't he!"

"I don't think that dog's housebroken," the pilot said as the first passenger appeared in the doorway.

A huge woman slowly squeezed herself out of the plane and eyed the dock nervously. Richard and the pilot reached for her hands and hauled her to safety. She was followed by a corpulent man with a wooden leg. Panting and wheezing, he wedged himself in the doorway and slowly lowered his good leg to the pontoon. The plane listed to one side.

"Back! Back!" the corpulent man called to the third passenger, who had moved to the pilot's seat and was attempting to look out the door. Again Richard and the pilot reached out and hauled Martinette's guest to the dock.

The last passenger was the biggest of all. He was so obese he could barely squeeze himself through the door. But he seemed more agile than the other two, and didn't need help to step off the plane.

Martinette guided her three tourists and their dog up the hill to the resort hotel while Richard and I rowed back home. We could hear the dog yapping as we crossed the bay.

"We're going to need some repairs over here," Richard remarked as we approached our jetty. It was true. At low tide especially the ramp was terrifically dangerous, descending at a slick fifty degree angle. The whole ramshackle affair tilted to port on account of a sunken buoyancy chamber. Every once in a while at a very low tide the dock would get caught on the pilings, rotted and encrusted with a slimy variety of shellfish, and then it would tilt even further.

A metal grill had been nailed to the slippery boards to give some traction during rainy weather, but it was no longer securely fastened down. Rusty little spikes and sharp corners reached up to trip the unwary.

Frank Weston was well aware of the state of the jetty, but he said it wasn't a School Board responsibility. According to the Board office, the Parks Department would have to initiate any repairs. We'd asked for an address to write to, hoping to expedite the process, but the School Board said that they'd take care of it. All we could do was hope that it would be fixed before one of our students was seriously hurt.

Chapter Twenty

The Last Resort

We were glad of the week-long holiday at March Break. Teaching had become more and more unrewarding and stressful, and we all wanted to get away.

For a change we took the *Anna Magdalena* to Port Hardy, the closest thing to a "big city" on the north island. Deciding that money was no object, we took taxis when we wanted to go somewhere, taking full advantage of the amenities the town could offer. We went to movies and ice cream parlors, bought books and new clothes, and treated ourselves to several restaurant meals. By the time we arrived back in Blubber Bay we were feeling much cheered and refreshed.

I didn't think anything of it when the Davidson children didn't turn up after the March Break. Their attendance was usually good, but every once in a while the boat didn't come from the reservation. However this absence stretched into days, then finally a week.

Rainbow came to see me on Friday after school.

"Maggie Edenshaw came by today. She stayed so she could take Patsy home with her. Timothy is dead. We just found out. He hanged himself during the holidays."

Dead! I felt as if a rock had lodged in my chest. It would stay there for days.

"Patrick found him. It happened in their bedroom, while the others were out. He tied a rope to the overhead light."

"My god. Those poor kids."

Rainbow came to school on Monday morning to help Richard and me break the news to our students. Most of them knew it by then, but we still spent hours talking about Timothy and trying to make sense of the tragedy.

I encouraged the children to write about their feelings and memories, and to express themselves in artwork. We packaged up some of the more caring and sensitive results to send to Timothy's mother.

Patrick and Jason never came back to school. I tried writing to them, and mailed the cards at Martinette's store. Eventually we heard that they had moved to Alert Bay, and were going to school there.

Teaching is probably the most rewarding profession there is, but also the most tragic. We try so hard to make a difference, but sometimes an education is not what kids need most.

#

As the weather warmed up, ants invaded the trailer. We'd always had mice, but ants were something new.

The first day I noticed a couple scurrying by my armchair as I read to Donna after supper. The next evening, dozens were strolling over the kitchen counter. By the day after that, we were seriously under siege.

A swarm of ants covered the can of corn syrup in the cupboard. They poured from cracks in the wall and from beneath the fridge. I submerged the syrup can in the sink and massacred dozens as they lapped up a splash of juice on the floor.

Under other circumstances I might have thought them rather cute. Pert little honey-brown creatures, they were rather pretty as ants go. But they were soon joined by brutish black cousins, some of whom gave a nasty bite when cornered.

Richard bought ant traps and poison at Martinette's store, but it was weeks before we got rid of the last of them, and I don't think the insecticides really did much good. It was the daily, unremitting slaughter that finally got their numbers under control.

#

By this time I had been forced to recognize that the school curriculum and rules of conduct were regarded by many children and parents as my personal idiosyncracies rather than as provincial norms. Stephanie was sure that she was the only student who'd ever been forced to learn times tables, while Ricky Hill could not see the sense of cursive writing or learning to use a dictionary.

Aside from Hans and Donna, none of these children had ever attended a conventional city school. They were unaware that large numbers of children all over the country were doing these very things, progressing through the cumulative steps of their education year after year, and they felt very isolated and hard done by. I tried remedying the problem by borrowing 16 millimeter movie films from the National Film Board in Vancouver, and reading aloud stories that would show children in regular classrooms, but nothing seemed to help. More and more of my students were developing a belief that they were the only children in the world who had to write in journals, produce book reports, and complete math assignments.

I tried to structure my teaching units around themes that grew out of the kids' own enthusiasms. In the first year that had been easy. Whales, wolves, fishing, the oceans . . . we were excited about so many things that we never ran out of ideas to study. But by the second wet spring, even the most cooperative kids were feeling disenchanted. Kids like Sylvain Lemieux, Patsy Edenshaw and Garth Campbell continued to work from a sense of loyalty and duty, but even they couldn't maintain the atmosphere of curiosity and adventure that belongs in a classroom. Instead of inspiring a love of learning I was starting to feel like a prison warden.

One rainy day the kids had free time in the classroom after

eating their lunches. Some of them read or drew, while others played a game of monopoly on the carpet. I listened to their conversation as I marked language arts assignments.

"I wonder if we'll have a different teacher next year," Lindsay Campbell mused as she moved her marker around the board. "Mom says we've never had the same teacher for longer than two years."

"Do you think Mr. Hartman would come back?" Veronica was remembering the teacher who had preceded me.

"I hope that Mercy will be our next teacher," said Lisa. "My mom likes her."

"I like Mercy too," said Laverne. "She makes great pies and cinnamon buns. Maybe if she was our teacher she'd bring stuff to school."

"She probably would," Wilson assured them. "My Mom gives out candy and money when you're good."

The kids considered this.

"I think my mom *will* be the teacher," said little Bobby Goodman. I wondered whether the comment came from his own desire, or whether he'd overheard adults discussing the matter at home.

#

A day or two after this, Ricky and Veronica Hill came to school looking very self satisfied. Veronica didn't say anything, but Ricky chortled, "My mom is going to get you. You'll see!"

I wondered what Charlotte was going to "get us" for. She'd always been so reasonable and friendly that I didn't worry much about Ricky's threats.

That afternoon Richard and I rowed over for the mail together. Martinette met us with a wide grin.

"So, you finally let the kid have it, eh?"

"What?" Richard looked as confused as I felt.

"Ricky Hill. The little brat has been telling everybody that you hit him. Well, I'm sure he deserved it."

"I didn't hit Ricky." I couldn't even think of a time when I'd put a hand on his shoulder to settle him down, or touched him in any way for the past several months.

"A good smack on the behind is what that kid needs. That's what I told Charlotte when she came whining to me."

"Charlotte is telling people that I hit Ricky?"

"She sure is. Charlotte and Giselle are trying to get you fired, but don't worry. Something like this happens to every teacher. It'll blow over."

I didn't feel reassured. We collected our mail and rowed for a while in silence.

Finally Richard said, "Honey, it might be time to consider moving on."

"You're right. I hate to let them win, but this is getting ridiculous. How could Charlotte believe that I'd hit anyone?"

"So many people *want* to hit Ricky Hill that they just can't believe anyone would pass up the chance. What bothers me more is that Veronica apparently backed him up."

"That's true. She must be lying too." I remembered what Veronica had said during their game of monopoly. Was she desperate enough for a new teacher that she'd resort to this kind of manipulation?

I phoned Frank, but he had already heard the news.

"Giselle Baker and Charlotte Hill both phoned the School Board this afternoon. I told the Board to cite the School Act and instruct them to write letters. I'll be over again soon."

Charlotte's defection made me feel much worse than the problems with other parents had done. On the other hand, there was no doubt that she believed her own children. I wished she would come and see me so that we could sort out the problem, but I only ever saw Charlotte once again.

#

Throughout all this, Donna had pretty much kept her thoughts to herself. She complained sometimes about Hans or the twins, and she was aware of the rumors that poisoned the community, but Rainbow Hurley and Paddy Potter helped us shelter Donna from the worst of it by making her welcome whenever she needed a break from the school and the teacherage.

The year had been difficult for her too. Besides the limited social life, Donna was often tormented by the other children because her mother was the teacher. Any time the students felt that I was too strict or they were unhappy with a decision I had made, they would take it out on Donna. At the same time her good marks were attributed to favoritism, and while I scolded and disciplined her as I would anyone else, many parents as well as their children believed that I'd let Donna get away with anything.

Around that time Donna wrote an entry in her school journal that showed her feelings very clearly:

> Suppose you were never allowed to leave your house and yard for three or four months at a time. Suppose you could never walk to the corner store or make phone calls to your friends or go to a movie. Wouldn't that seem like jail?
>
> And suppose you couldn't get mail or fresh groceries for days at a time. What if on your few days of freedom every three or four months you had to pack in all the errands, appointments, shopping, and visiting that you'd normally stretch out through that whole period. Wouldn't that seem pretty hard?
>
> And suppose it rained a great deal and you had no T.V. and a very limited supply of fresh books or music. And that you had only two friends, and one of them you could never see except in school. And all of the other kids hate you.
>
> Wouldn't you wonder what you had done to deserve this?

The next day I phoned Frank Weston and tendered my resignation. I explained that Donna's unhappiness was the last straw. In any case, Donna needed to be back in the city and preparing herself to go to high school.

Richard and I were not sure whether it would be wiser to keep this decision to ourselves, or to let the community know that we'd be leaving. Finally we decided on the latter course. For one thing we hoped that Charlotte, Giselle, Mrs. Campbell and Mrs. Potts would stop fighting if they knew there was no further need to drive us away. For another, we didn't want Donna to have to keep this secret. She'd often proved that she could be discrete, but why bother?

#

As we'd hoped, pressure and conflict eased almost immediately. Charlotte made an effusive visit to the school to tell me how sorry she was that we were leaving. Other people made more sincere comments to the same effect. The Hurleys and Lemieux's seemed genuinely grieved to hear the news.

Ironically, once the first novelty had worn off, the students stopped anticipating their change in teachers with glee, and began to cling to the old and familiar. The Campbell girls insisted that I was the best teacher they'd ever had, and I received several cards and drawings from different members of the class addressed to "My Favorite Teacher."

A week later Giselle moved to Campbell River taking not only Hans, but Nancy with her as well. Without fanfare or explanation the three of them packed their bags and boarded a Cessna that was leaving from the resort.

We started rehearsing *A Midsummer Night's Dream* to present at the end of the year, and held our Annual Nettle Feast a little later than usual. The last two months of school passed so peacefully and productively that the earlier enmities and discipline problems seemed like a bad dream.

At our Track-and-Field Event on the last day of school, Mercy Goodman presented us with a gift from the community. It was a large painting of Blubber Bay School that she had copied from a snapshot.

\#

There were many people we would regret leaving behind. Summer Sunshine was a gifted and beautiful child, able to keep up with the older students in any subject. Wilson Goodman had learning disabilities, but he was an outstanding artist and a keen story-teller. Sylvain Lemieux had great musical gifts as well as being a talented scholar and athlete. And Garth Campbell was a "great heart" who never took part in his sisters' machinations.

We would miss the Potters, and George and Sylvia Goodman. During all those months of gossip and moral leprosy they had remained dependable and true.

As we motored out of Blubber Bay for the last time and turned the bow of the *Anna Magdalena* to the south we watched the white shell beach and the floathouses disappear behind the headland. We had no regrets. In a week we would be in Victoria. In a week life would start anew.

Appendix

Student Lists

First Year (1982-1983)		*Second Year (1983-1984)*	
Danny Storto	grade 8	(dropped out)	
Bradley Hicks (January-May)	grade 7	(moved away)	
Angelica Davidson	grade 6	(moved to Alert Bay)	
Patrick Davidson	grade 6	Patrick Davidson	grade 7
Helen Potts	grade 6	Helen Potts	grade 7
Hans Baker	grade 5	Hans Baker	grade 6
Lisa Campbell	grade 5	Lisa Campbell	grade 6
Veronica Hill	grade 5	Veronica Hill	grade 6
Stephanie Potts	grade 5	Stephanie Potts	grade 6
Donna Todd	grade 5	Donna Todd	grade 6
Garth Campbell	grade 4	Garth Campbell	grade 5
Laverne Campbell	grade 4	Laverne Campbell	grade 5
Lindsay Campbell	grade 4	Lindsay Campbell	grade 5
Timothy Davidson	grade 4	Timothy Davidson	grade 5
Patsy Edenshaw	grade 4	Patsy Edenshaw	grade 5
Wilson Goodman	grade 4	Wilson Goodman	grade 5
Sylvain Lemieux	grade 4	Sylvain Lemieux	grade 5
Derrick Hicks (January-May)	grade 4	(moved away)	
Summer Sunshine Hurley	grade 3	Summer Sunshine Hurley	grade 4
Jason Davidson	grade 2	Jason Davidson	grade 3
Ricky Hill	grade 2	Ricky Hill	grade 3
Davy Campbell	grade K	Davy Campbell	grade 1
		Autumn Mist Hurley	grade K
		Bobby Goodman	grade K

BVG